"You were wond[erful]"

Tara spoke in a dreamy voice as she lifted her hand to touch Gage. "It was the most—"

"Please," he interrupted, his voice deliberately offhand in a panicked effort to stop her before she made more out of their night together than it was supposed to be. "If you say any more, I'll blush."

Tara's expression cooled in an instant. Her fingers, as they lifted the damp hair off of his forehead, were suddenly more casual than tender. "A Kingston *blush?*" She gave his hair a flick with her fingers before dropping her hand to the mattress between them. "I'd like to get that on film."

"Film?"

"There are people who'd pay good money to see it," she said flippantly. She yawned extravagantly and glanced at the small clock on the nightstand. "It's been fun, but I really have to get my beauty sleep." She yawned again. "Lock the door on your way out, would you?"

Without a word, Gage quickly dressed. As instructed, he closed and locked the door with exaggerated care, fighting the urge to slam it hard enough to break the glass.

He'd been used!

Dear Reader,

I confess. I'm a movie junkie. The habit started when I was a little kid. I'd spend my allowance on the Saturday matinee and sit through *both* features and the cartoons, at least twice. As an adult, one of my favorite indulgences is to see four or five movies over a weekend, either at the local cinema or cuddled up on the couch in front of my video machine. I'll watch just about any kind of movie—Western, action, science fiction, suspense, drama or, of course, romance.

I've always been equally intrigued with the processes and people who make the movies. I'm an avid reader of *People, Entertainment Weekly* and *Premiere,* I've read every actor's biography ever written and I found "The Making of *Terminator 2*" as spellbinding as the movie itself.

So, of course, I was *destined* to write about the Kingstons' Hollywood Dynasty.

The research was fascinating! I learned about storyboarding, gaffers, dolly grips, intercutting and the difference between a dissolve and a fade. Research also gave me a guilt-free reason to read all the supermarket tabloids—where I found out that nothing I could dream up for my Hollywood heroes and heroines could come *close* to what's printed about real-life movie stars.

So make yourself a big bowl of popcorn and curl up in your favorite reading spot. I hope you have as much fun reading about living and loving in Hollywood as I did writing about it.

Sincerely,

Candace Schuler

P.S. Don't forget to complete the questionnaire at the back of the book!

THE OTHER WOMAN

CANDACE SCHULER

Harlequin Books

TORONTO • NEW YORK • LONDON
AMSTERDAM • PARIS • SYDNEY • HAMBURG
STOCKHOLM • ATHENS • TOKYO • MILAN
MADRID • WARSAW • BUDAPEST • AUCKLAND

To my agent, Evan Marshall,
for his patience, tact and guidance

Published July 1993

ISBN 0-373-25551-9

THE OTHER WOMAN

1

SHE WAS EVE INCARNATE; soft, seductive temptation; warm, inviting womanflesh; every carnal delight he'd ever thought of or imagined. Just standing there, staring at her with half the width of the room between them was driving him crazy with mind-numbing desires.

The creamy smooth curve of her shoulder above the thin blanket, the seductive dip of her waist, the promising swell of her hip outlined beneath the faded blue wool made his palms tingle with the need to touch her. The firelight flickering on the reddish glints in her luxuriant honey-colored hair beckoned him forward to bury his face in her silky curls. The way her slanted cat's eyes flared wide in recognition and desire fueled a need to see them close in passion under the onslaught of his kisses. Every curve, every inviting hollow and swell of her body called to him like a siren's song.

"You have come," she breathed. "At last." Her lips were luscious and inviting as they formed the words. Her enchantingly accented voice was ripe with the promise of all his desires fulfilled. "I knew you would come."

She lifted her arms, holding them out as she rolled onto her back. The threadbare blanket pulled tight over the swell of her breasts, revealing the outline of her nipples and the faint sprinkling of freckles in her lush cleavage. He imagined kissing each and every one, drawing the loving out, making it last until she begged for completion.

And then she sat up and the blanket slid down, revealing her breasts in all their womanly glory. They were full, high and round, perfect globes of sweet feminine flesh, appearing almost too lush for the fragility of her narrow rib cage and straight, smooth shoulders. They were tipped with hard, mouth-watering little nipples of deep strawberry red and they trembled, ever so slightly, with the force of her arousal.

Gage felt his body begin to harden and he knew, beyond a shadow of a doubt, that she had the power to make him beg. He was already halfway there, inches away from reaching out for her...

"Cut!" the director hollered as laughter burst out all around.

It took him a moment to realize it wasn't directed at him, and then another to be thankful it had broken the spell she'd woven around his senses. Despite his years in the movie business, he'd gotten so wrapped up in the fantasy she'd created that he'd come *that close* to completely forgetting he was behind the camera on a remote movie set in Montana in the middle of one of the coldest winters on record, instead of alone with her in a bedroom. Another moment and he'd have done something even more stupid than getting mentally carried away by her acting.

"Cut, damn it!" yelled Hans Ostfield, the director, his voice carrying only the faintest hint of a Scandinavian accent as it boomed across the set. "Pierce, you ass—" he said, scowling through his laughter "—can't you ever be serious?"

It was a rhetorical question. Pierce Kingston, macho movie star, was rarely serious about anything. Disrupting the first critical scene of a new movie by sticking a grinning yellow happy face on the left cheek of his buttocks was about par for the course.

Through the lens of his camera, Gage Kingston watched his superstar brother bow to the laughing crew before calmly reaching down to pull his pants back up. Pierce was pure grade-A ham to the bone, as comfortable in front of the camera as he was in the privacy of his own home. Gage watched him with brotherly pride for a moment before his gaze was drawn inexorably back to the woman on the bed.

She'd yanked the blanket back up to cover her breasts and was staring at the grinning Pierce as if she couldn't decide whether to curse him or thank him. True, he'd lightened the tension on the set, drawing everyone's attention from her to him, but now the scene would have to be shot all over again. Which meant Tara Channing would have to bare her magnificent breasts again.

Gage wondered why it bothered her. Peering at her through the powerful lens of his camera, he could tell, quite clearly—*now*—that the trembling which had seemed so much like passion a moment ago was really due to nervousness. And that surprised him. She was, after all, an actress who'd played more love scenes than most. She'd built her career on a succession of seductive "other woman" roles—bimbos, *femme fatales*, villainnesses, Jezebels and adulterous sirens.

And there'd been those nude pictures a few years back in . . . what tabloid was it? Gage couldn't remember. One tabloid was the same as another, all flash, trash and sleazy nonsense. As a rule he didn't pay any attention to them but he *had* paid attention to the pictures of Tara Channing, just like every other normal red-blooded man in America.

It would have been hard not to.

Tara Channing was stunningly, impossibly, incredibly sexy. It wasn't just the cascading mass of luxuriantly thick, strawberry blond hair that tumbled past her shoulders, or her fantastic aquamarine eyes or even her magnificent body—although, Lord knew, she had a figure to make any Playmate of the Month weep with pea-green envy. It was something about the way that gorgeous mane of hair always looked so invitingly tousled, as if she wouldn't mind having it tousled even more. It was the way those huge eyes of hers were set above the classic purity of her cheekbones, slanted just enough so that every glance was effortlessly enticing. It was the way she held that magnificent body—the silent, seductive language that said, "Come and get me, I'm all yours"—that had males from sixteen to sixty drooling over themselves when they looked at her.

"It's the bones," Gage's mother, the legendary actress Elise Gage, had commented as the whole Kingston clan viewed a week's worth of the daytime drama Tara Channing was appearing in that season. She was one of a handful of young actresses, including Demi Moore and Winona Ryder, the family was considering offering the part of Pierce's doomed love interest in the next Kingston production—a political thriller set amidst the chaos created by the break-up of the former Soviet Union. "Ms. Channing has wonderful bones," Elise continued. "Simply wonderful. The youthful bloom will fade and gravity will do its evil work, as it does in all of us—"

"Except you," Gage's father, the equally legendary director, Barry Kingston, had said.

Elise had given her ex-husband a cool, narrow-eyed look that advised him to save his automatic gallantry for someone more susceptible to it, and kept on talking, "—but the bones will make her beautiful when she's seventy."

And his mother had been right. As a cameraman and one of the industry's leading cinematographers, Gage could see, quite clearly, that Tara Channing's bone structure would undoubtedly make her a lovely old lady. As a man, all he was really interested in at the moment was the luscious flesh covering those "wonderful" bones.

Would it be as soft as it looked? As warm? As giving?

"Will somebody get Ms. Channing her robe?" Hans hollered. "Her teeth are chattering. Arlo—" Arlo was a gangly young gofer, specifically employed to fetch and carry for the more important personalities on the set. "Ms. Channing needs her robe." When the young man failed to present himself immediately, Hans bellowed, "Where the hell is Arlo?" obviously forgetting that he himself had closed the set to any but essential personnel for this semi-nude love scene. All others had been banished to other regions of the huge barn they were using for the interior shots. "Somebody tell Arlo to get his scrawny ass in here, on the double," Hans barked. He reached out and patted Tara's shoulder. "We'll have your robe here in a minute, dear," he said absently, already turning to converse with his assistant director, who hovered at his elbow with a clipboard of lists and shooting schedules.

"Here, sweetheart." The irresistibly irrepressible Pierce dropped down onto the bed beside the blanket-draped actress and wrapped a bare brawny arm around her equally bare shoulders. "I'll keep you warm until they find your robe," he said, rubbing his hand up and down the gooseflesh on her shapely biceps. "I'm America's hottest actor, you know." He flashed the same meltingly sweet, sinfully wicked, cocksure smile that had endeared him to impressionable women everywhere. "One look from these eyes will melt glaciers," he added, giving her what the tabloids termed his "patented laserlike gaze."

Still staring through the lens of his camera, Gage watched Tara Channing laugh at his brother's asinine remarks. He watched her lashes lower and lift flirtatiously, giving Pierce the little sidelong glance she was known for. He watched her mouth move next to his brother's ear, saying something that made Pierce laugh in turn.

Well, hell, Gage thought, shaking his head with mild disgust. *Here we go again.*

The sexy Ms. Channing evidently knew all about Pierce's legendary weakness for the ladies and, from the looks of things, she was fully prepared to exploit it to her advantage. What she probably didn't know was that cozying up to a Kingston—even softhearted, soft-headed Pierce Kingston—didn't automatically garner an actress any special career considerations at Kingston Productions. Or maybe, Gage thought, she did know but figured that what she had to offer was so special she would be the exception.

And then he saw the slight stiffening of her body as Pierce's teasing brought all eyes to the bed again, and the way she somehow managed to slip out of Pierce's loose embrace without appearing to move at all.

She doesn't like all the attention, Gage thought incredulously. He shook his head. *Nonsense, she's an actress.*

Attention was as vital to actors and actresses as the air they breathed. They lived for attention and, more often than not, pouted when it wasn't immediately forthcoming. But Tara Channing wasn't pouting. And unlike he'd first thought, she wasn't posturing or play-acting or even really participating in any of the good-natured ribbing going on between Pierce and the crew. She was . . . cringing.

Was it possible?

Gage zoomed in for a tighter shot to confirm it. Yes, she was definitely cringing, he decided, staring at the breathtakingly beautiful face filling up his monitor. Her eyes held just a touch of unease; her lips were pressed together just a bit too tightly; there was a faint line between her arched brows.

What the hell?

He leaned back and sideways, looking around the edge of the camera, trying to understand why no one else seemed to notice that the woman on the bed looked as if she'd rather be anyplace other than where she was.

The reason was immediately obvious. Without the powerful lens of his camera magnifying every nuance of her expression, she didn't look the least bit uneasy sitting practically naked in the middle of an unmade bed with a bare-chested man beside her and another half-a-dozen fully clad people bustling around her.

She looked cool and confident and as sexy as hell.

Gage shook his head, deciding he'd been seeing things; actresses didn't shy from attention, they demanded it. And then he looked back into his camera again, just as the young gofer came around the corner of the makeshift bedroom wall with Tara's robe over his arm. The look that flashed in the actress's expressive eyes made Gage think of a drowning victim who'd spotted a life preserver.

Before he could think to stop himself, Gage moved from behind the camera. "Here, Arlo, I'll take that," he said, grabbing the robe. "You get out of here before Hans catches sight of you."

The gofer released the robe and backed away from the walled-off area with a wistful glance at the bed, obviously torn between the need to avoid the wrath of the irate director and the all-to-rare opportunity to ogle a bona fide sex symbol in the flesh.

Gage didn't even notice the young man's retreat; his eyes were on Tara's face, trying to decipher the intriguing puzzle of emotions he alone saw there. In four steps, over cables, past the klieg lights and around the busy, bustling crew, he was kneeling on the low-slung bed, dropping a blue velour robe over Tara's beautiful shoulders.

She looked up at him from under her lashes, giving him the brief, seductive glance out of the corners of her eyes that seemed to be second nature to her. "Thank you," she said softly, her voice entirely free of the Slavic accent she'd spoken with while the cameras were rolling. She reached up with one hand to pull the comforting folds of the robe around her.

To anyone else, it must have looked as if she were merely snuggling into the warmth. To Gage, who'd seen the flash of relief and gratitude in her eyes when she'd seen the robe, it looked very much as if she were trying to hide herself in the bulky material. Looming over her, looking down, he could see individual strands of her tumbled golden red hair, the soft shadow of her lashes on her cheek, and the creamy skin of her upper chest just above where her hand clutched the lapels of her robe together. She had a few very faint freckles on the back of her hand, matching those scattered across her cleavage.

Gage wondered what she'd do if he leaned down and kissed them. The ones on her hand first, and then up her arm—she must, he thought, have a few freckles on her arm—until his lips reached the ones on her breasts. *Would she murmur softly?* he wondered, swaying a bit closer in an unconscious effort to breathe in the seductive scent of her hair. *Would she tilt her head back to give him better access? Would she—*

"Damn it, Gage, what the hell are you doing over there?" Hans growled. The fact that he was shooting a Kingston Production, with Gage Kingston as his cinematographer and Pierce Kingston as his leading man, impressed him not a whit. He was the director and on the set his word was law. "We're ready to start shooting again. That is," he added, scowling at the trio on the bed, "if you and Pierce can manage to quit acting like a couple of horny jackasses and get your minds back on business."

Gage looked up quickly, meeting his brother's eyes over the fragrant strawberry blond head between them. He hadn't realized they were hovering above her. But they were—like two dogs over a particularly meaty bone. Tara blinked, her wide-eyed, slanted gaze flitting questioningly from one handsome face to the other. Pierce preened, grinning like the rascal he was. Gage, to his horror, very nearly blushed.

He yanked himself back, jerking his knee off the bed, and strode to his camera, angry at himself for his uncharacteristic lack of control.

"Come on, Pierce," Hans ordered when the actor paused to lift Tara's hand to his lips. "Quit your horsing around and move it." He jerked his thumb toward the false door through which Pierce would make his entrance. "And take that damn silly thing off your butt before you come out here again."

"Places, everybody," hollered the assistant director as Pierce obligingly disappeared behind the prop door. Tara handed her robe to a waiting crew member from Wardrobe and slid back into position in the bed. "Quiet on the set."

"Roll film," Hans instructed, "and..." the clapper came down for take two "...action."

The scene went smoothly this time, letter-perfect from the moment the woman on the bed became aware of her lover's presence, to the moment when he covered her body with his and their lips met in a searing openmouthed kiss.

"Cut and print," Hans said. "Good job, people. Really splendid." He grinned at Pierce and Tara as they shrugged into their robes. "You two are going to burn up the damned screen. Hot stuff."

Pierce inclined his head in regal acknowledgment.

Tara smiled in relief.

Gage stood stock-still behind his camera, torn between professional admiration at the way Tara had taken her nervousness and turned it into a flawless simulation of red-hot passion and quite unprofessional amazement at the jealousy churning through him.

No, not jealousy, he quickly corrected himself. The emotion that had tightened his gut while filming the love scene between his brother and Tara Channing was envy, pure and simple.

Well, maybe not so pure, he amended, tugging surreptitiously at the suddenly too-tight front of his jeans.

What red-blooded man wouldn't be envious watching Pierce make love—even pretend love—to a woman as beautiful and sexy as Tara Channing? There'd have to be something wrong with any man who didn't feel at least a twinge of envy. Even a saint would be envious. And no one had ever accused Gage Kingston of bucking for sainthood. Even now, he was still imagining *his* chest pressed against Tara's bare breasts, *his* mouth tasting hers.

He watched her rise from the bed, with the midcalf blue robe wrapped snugly around her, looking deliciously tousled and bedwarmed, and wondered if her publicity was true or, rather, how *much* of it was true. Was she really the heartless *femme fatale* depicted in the tabloids? The notorious "other woman" offscreen as well as on?

He knew from the vast experience of a lifetime spent in the unwelcome glare of Hollywood publicity that the scandal sheets routinely exaggerated and quite often created stories out of whole cloth in their never-ending quest to sell papers. He also knew, however, there was often a nugget of truth buried in a lot of the stories that were printed.

His parents, for instance, hadn't engaged in nearly as many public marital brawls as the tabloids would have the world believe. But they *had* fought—more often and more loudly than any of their three children would have liked. And although Pierce couldn't possibly have been involved with all the women he'd been linked with in print—"I am, after all, only a mortal man," he'd said more than once—he'd been involved with enough women for Gage to know his reputation as a consummate ladies' man wasn't completely undeserved. And then, of course, there was Gage's own nasty brush with tabloid fame when his ex-wife had decided to take their very messy divorce public. Although Alyssa had embellished the facts, adding a few titillating and entirely false details to put herself in a better light, the bare bones of the story had been painfully true.

Besides, even without what could be—and, to be fair, probably *were*—totally fabricated tabloid stories about the sexy Ms. Channing, there were still those nude photos that had been published a few years ago. They certainly hadn't been snapped while she was sunbathing, unaware of the camera invading her privacy. She'd posed for them, deliberately baring her spectacular body for the sake of publicity.

Not that he was so provincial as to think there was anything wrong with nudity. His younger sister Claire had done a nude love scene before she'd decided producing movies was more to her taste than starring in them. Pierce, ham that he was, thought nothing of dropping his drawers if doing so was crucial to the screenplay. Hell, he'd even seen an old movie still of his mother wearing little more than a smile and a few strategic bits of black lace. It was just a part of the business. It meant nothing, less than nothing, really, and yet.... There was a part of him, admittedly oldfashioned and chauvinistic, that couldn't quite get over the notion that the frequency and casualness with which his ex-wife shed her clothes on screen for the sake of her career was an indication of how easily she removed them offscreen for the same cause.

Not that Tara Channing peeled down to her skin with the same blasé indifference Alyssa always displayed. Or, at least, she didn't seem to, but still . . .

Gage let his gaze wander over to where Tara sat, perched on a high canvas-backed stool in front of an electric space heater, being primped and fussed over like a Barbie doll. Her chin was raised, her lips parted slightly to facilitate the makeup artist's lip brush. Her head was tilted back to accommodate the woman who was fluffing her hair. Her wide, slanted eyes were serious and respectful as she listened to Hans explain what facets of her character's personality and mood he wanted emphasized in the reaction shots. Her feet were braced on the middle rung of the stool, her left leg bared to midthigh where the robe had fallen away.

So, Gage mused, was the real Tara Channing the sexually sophisticated, coolly conniving "other woman" of the tabloids who wouldn't really care which Kingston brother she cozied up to if it helped her career? Was she the engagingly nervous woman who'd reluctantly bared her breasts to his camera for the sake of the screenplay? Or was she someone else altogether?

He ran his gaze down the creamy length of her bared leg, imagining it in any number of positions that included close contact with himself, and decided it was of monumental importance that he find out as soon as possible.

As SHE LISTENED TO HANS tell her what she already knew about her character's motivation, Tara surreptitiously watched Gage Kingston watch her and felt a sinking sensation in the pit of her stomach. She recognized the look in his hot amber eyes.

Recognized it and dreaded it.

It was the same look too many men had been giving her since she'd turned fourteen and suddenly needed bust darts on all her blouses. It was a blatantly sexual look, full of masculine speculation and appraisal, as assessing as if she were standing on an auction block.

Does she or doesn't she?

Will she or won't she?

When she was fourteen that look had confused her, making her uneasy without knowing exactly why, and she'd turned away from it whenever it was directed at her. When she was seventeen, she'd thought it meant love and acceptance and she'd quit turning away, turning instead into the arms of the ardent young man whose hungry eyes had followed her every move. By the time she was seventeen-and-a-half, she'd discovered it meant pain and betrayal and she'd run from it, as far and as fast as she could, vowing to never let it hurt her again.

It had taken another hard knock or two to really drive the lesson home, teaching her there were variations on the look and confirming what she'd learned of its dangers. Now, at twenty-five, she finally knew exactly what the look meant and, more importantly, she knew how to handle it.

Publicly, she parried it with a cool, confident look of her own. One that said "Wouldn't you like to know?" to any man whose eyes asked if her lush body was matched by a passionate nature.

Privately, she ignored it.

Completely.

Absolutely.

No exceptions.

Ever.

It had always seemed to be the best defense and, yet, somehow, despite her attitude—or, she sometimes morosely thought, maybe because of it—she'd been linked to this director and that producer and almost every actor she'd ever done a love scene with. And quite a few she hadn't. The nude pictures had been bad enough, but she'd been halfway prepared for those—

some part of her had known her sleazy ex-agent would release them despite her protests. She'd been angry but stoic. She'd posed for the pictures, however reluctantly, and it served her right to have them splashed all over the tabloids.

But she didn't deserve the stories that came later.

The first time the press had labeled her the "other woman" in some actor's messy divorce, she'd dissolved into angry, disbelieving tears, wondering out loud how they could print trash like that when there was absolutely no truth to it. Her new agent, a practical, levelheaded woman who'd been in the business for more years than she would admit to, had advised Tara to forget it. "Your denials will just add fuel to the fire," Margo had counseled. "Just forget it and go on with your life."

So Tara had forgotten it—or tried to. Just like she'd tried to forget all the other things she'd been called since then, both in print and in private. Home wrecker. Ball buster. Bitch-goddess. Tease. One well-known lothario, outraged when she'd declined the honor of becoming his latest conquest, had even suggested she probably preferred women. The words still hurt—they always hurt, no matter who said them or how untrue they were—but Tara had gradually learned they were useful, too, keeping all but the most egotistical men at a safe distance.

So, she wondered, covertly eyeing her admirer, *how much of an ego does Gage Kingston have?*

If she were really lucky he would prove to be one of that most rare of the male species—a reasonable man. Then, ego or no ego, it would only take a few gentle rebuffs before he got the message that, despite her looks and her media image, she wasn't interested in becoming his location playmate.

She hoped she was going to be lucky.

She liked his brother.

She'd felt something for Pierce Kingston the moment she'd looked up into his impossibly handsome face just before the audition that had ultimately landed her the part of Yelena Zdravkovich. Oh, not the kind of feeling the tabloids were already reporting on, but a kinship of sorts. They'd shaken hands and smiled at each other—two wildly glamorous, outrageously beautiful human beings, both blessed and burdened with all the excess baggage of being a sexual ideal, with nothing to prove to each other and not even a spark of sexual attraction between them—and then played the scene with enough smoldering heat to melt celluloid, just like the competent professionals they were.

"Let's be friends and drive everybody crazy," Pierce had said when it was over. And Tara had agreed, feeling as if she'd suddenly found a brother. She didn't want to jeopardize her budding friendship with Pierce—not to mention the most important role of her career—by having to shoot down his older brother's ego. But she would if she had to. She sent Gage another furtive glance from under her lashes.

And if she could.

He was almost as gorgeous as his superstar brother. They were nearly the same height, with Gage just a bit shorter than the six-foot-three inches listed in his brother's official bio. They had the same broad-shouldered, slim-hipped, long-legged, rangy-and-rugged cowboy build that looked as good in unforgivingly tight blue jeans as it did in a business suit. They had the same loose-limbed way of moving. They even had the same easy, engaging grin that showed lots of strong white teeth.

But instead of the thick, sun-streaked mane of blond hair that covered Pierce's finely shaped head, Gage's hair was a deep sable brown and he wore it shorter, its curling ends ruthlessly brushed into smooth submission against the back of his skull. Instead of the pure, chiseled features that gave Pierce a face to rival Michelangelo's *David*, Gage had a more rugged, lived-in look, like a man who'd spent his days on the back of a horse or at the bow of a ship, squinting into the sun.

Gage lacked the small, hidden dimple that flashed each time his brother smiled. He had a small scar instead, a curving arc that sliced through his left eyebrow, and his nose, if she wasn't mistaken, had been broken once upon a time, leaving a shallow dent across the bridge that made him look a bit lawless and slightly more . . . dangerous, she decided, than Pierce.

The biggest difference, though, was in the brothers' eyes. Pierce's eyes were as clear and blue as the summer sky, full of deliciously wicked secrets and warm, inviting laughter. Gage's eyes were an unusual light golden brown—inherited from his famous mother—that gleamed like highly polished amber. Their habitual expression was intense and focused, revealing a fierce sensuality and an iron will that made him seem somehow more—the word came to her again—*dangerous*. Dangerous to her, mainly.

Dangerous because, for the first time in more years than she cared to count, she actually felt the tiniest, teeniest, *scariest* bit like returning the look in Gage Kingston's hotly assessing amber eyes.

2

TARA SHIFTED UNEASILY in her canvas-backed chair, trying to avoid acknowledging that—after two days of sending out unmistakable I'm-not-the-least-bit-interested signals like mad—she was *still* being stared at by a man who made no effort to hide what he was doing even though, at the moment, he had absolutely no excuse for doing it.

Shooting had come to a screeching standstill almost fifteen minutes ago because the young actor playing the movie's post-communist radical wasn't satisfied with the direction he was getting from Hans. Jeremy Dean had been rescued from the obscurity of a string of low-budget horror movies to play the part of a provincial young Russian thrust headlong into the confusion created by the dissolution of the Soviet Union. Instead of being abjectly grateful for the chance he'd been offered, Jeremy kept trying to tell Hans how *he* thought the role should be interpreted.

The two of them were arguing loudly and dramatically over the character's motivation. Or, rather, Jeremy Dean was arguing loudly and dramatically over motivation. Hans Ostfield was standing with his hands on his hips, his gray head cocked and his expression impassive, reminding Tara of an old bear listening to the self-indulgent caterwauling of a cub. So far, he'd let the intense young actor emote to his heart's content but everybody on the set knew, except Jeremy apparently, that Hans's tolerance for artistic temperament had very definite limits. Limits that anyone with more than two brain cells—or a less massively insecure ego—could see had just about been reached.

Characteristically, Pierce had immediately absented himself from the area of conflict, obviously seeing the unscheduled break in shooting as an opportunity to flirt with the head electrician's Best Boy, who in this case was very much a woman. Tara had escaped to what she'd hoped would be a few minutes of anonymity. She'd positioned herself behind the cameras and the glare of the klieg lights, well out of the range of Gage Kingston's zoom lens and as close to a heater as possible. She was trying, quite unsuccessfully, to lose herself in the pages of one of the weightier books on her self-imposed, self-improving reading list. Most of the rest of the cast and crew had formed a loosely structured ring around the combatants, waiting with ill-concealed glee for the fireworks.

Except for Gage.

He stood with his back to the incipient action, his arms crossed over his chest, one broad shoulder propped up against his camera, and stared. The intensity of his gaze rattled her all the way down to her bones, leaving absolutely no doubt in *her* mind as to what he had on *his*.

Tara suppressed a shiver that mixed an unfamiliar but strangely delicious anticipation with awful dread. She turned another unread page of her book, trying to appear as if she didn't notice the man who was so brazenly, blatantly, noticing her. Maybe if she continued refusing to acknowledge him, just completely ignored him, he'd stop. But he didn't. In fact, her indifference only seemed to spur him to action.

Without actually looking at him, Tara saw him push himself away from his camera with a flex of his shoulders and move toward her with the intent, focused air of a predator who'd just scented fresh blood.

Hers.

Oh, no, she thought, her gaze glued to the pages of her book. *He's coming over here!*

She felt perspiration break out on her palms and she tightened her fingers on the leather-bound pasteboard cover in her lap, resisting the urge to wipe her hands against the drab wool skirt of her costume. She hadn't felt this fluttery and anxious since Bobby Clay Bishop had taken to staring at her in eleventh-grade Chemistry class back in Clayville, Texas. Worse, she had the sinking feeling that she wasn't going to handle this particular male any better than she'd handled her first one.

Somehow she knew the hard-won hint of aloofness, the carefully cultivated indifference that worked with most men wasn't going to be enough to warn off Gage Kingston any more than her naiveté and innocence had kept bad Bobby Clay at bay when she was seventeen. A wolf, after all, didn't stop stalking a fawn because the fawn was unaware or uninterested in becoming its next meal.

Still, she was determined to try, and not only because of her nascent friendship with the wolf's brother. Common sense alone told her that an angry, insulted Kingston wouldn't do much for harmony on the set or for her possible future with Kingston Productions. Knowing she had to play it calm and cool, Tara took a deep breath and waited for Gage Kingston's opening salvo. She didn't have to wait long.

"The tabloids would never believe it."

Willing herself not to start at the sound of his voice, Tara glanced up with a smile of greeting on her face and then deliberately let it dim a calculated degree or two, as if she'd been ready to welcome an interruption but was disappointed to discover it had come in the form of Gage Kingston. "The tabloids would never believe what?" she asked coolly, trying to sound totally disinterested.

"You." Gage dropped his long, lean, denim-clad frame into the canvas-backed chair with his brother's name scrawled across the back and nodded at the heavy hardbound book in Tara's lap. "Reading that," he said, stretching his booted feet toward the heater.

Tara gave him a sideways glance, one with more than a hint of aloofness in it. "Would it fit your image of me better if I said I only look at the pictures?"

Gage grinned at her, not the least put off. "It might if there were any pictures."

She flipped a page and tilted the book, showing him a line drawing of an Arab sheik labeled "Auda Abu Tayi."

Gage didn't even glance at it. "I was thinking more of the centerfold variety," he said, without taking his eyes off her face. There was a wealth of innuendo and masculine speculation in his warm amber gaze.

Tara's eyes hardened without any calculation at all. How she hated that look! "Most men do," she said tartly, and turned back to the musty account of T. E. Lawrence's adventures in Arabia.

It was as pointed a snub as Gage had ever been given, delivered with all the frigid politeness of a princess who'd been less than amused by the vulgar antics of the court jester. He stared at her bent head, hovering between impressed approval and disgruntled annoyance. On the one hand, he'd always liked a woman who could give as good as she got without turning a well-coiffed hair; his mother could freeze a man with a glance, offscreen as well as on, and his sister wasn't called the Ice Queen by the tabloids for nothing. On the other hand, he disliked—intensely, he'd just discovered—being so easily dismissed by a woman he was interested in. Even if he was only interested in getting her into bed.

Thoroughly vexed, Gage slouched down in his brother's chair, crossed his right ankle over his left knee in a deliberately casual pose and brooded about Tara's unequivocal rebuff of his first subtle come-on. *Well, okay, maybe it hadn't exactly been subtle*, he thought. *But it hadn't been all that crass, either.*

The atmosphere on a movie set could get awfully bawdy and blue, especially on a remote location site. Long hours, boredom and isolation made the cast and crew desperate for any entertainment, no matter how lowbrow. Any woman who couldn't counter a mild come-on was in for a rocky time.

Except that she had countered it, he realized. And quite effectively, too. With a few cool words and a sharply slanted gaze she had all but cut him off at the knees.

Gage sank even lower in his chair, his elbows balanced on the wooden arms, his hands tented in front of his nose, scowling at Tara's averted face and wishing he was behind his camera. He seemed better able to get a more accurate fix on what she was feeling when her every expression was magnified by his zoom lens. He lifted his index fingers as if he were framing a shot and peered at her through them.

Damn, she's beautiful.

Her profile was almost childlike in its purity and yet deliciously erotic at the same time. The curve of her forehead was more serene than other women's, the short straight line of her nose more perfect, the delicate arch of her lips more lush, the sweep of those fabulous cheekbones more exotic, the softly pointed chin more enticingly feminine.

Nothing he wasn't used to, of course. He'd been around beautiful women since the day he was born.

Ava Gardner had been a frequent guest at his parents' palatial Beverly Hills home when Gage was a little boy; Elizabeth Taylor and Natalie Wood had attended parties there; women like Meryl Streep, Michelle Pfeiffer and Kim Basinger were his contemporaries and colleagues. Feminine beauty was commonplace in his life. No big deal.

He shifted in his seat, unconsciously trying to find a more comfortable position.

So why do I get so damned hot just looking at Tara Channing?

TARA SAT VERY STILL in her chair, her gaze glued to her book, desperately wishing he'd stop staring and go away. Couldn't the man take a hint? She didn't want him or his hot amber eyes or his clearly stated, if so far unspoken, intentions anywhere near her. It made her heart beat uncomfortably fast to have him so close. It made her palms sweat and her breath catch in her throat. It made her want to get up and run.

But she stayed right where she was, somehow instinctively knowing that to run, literally or figuratively, would only rouse the male beast in him and make him chase her harder. Most men were that way to some degree. Gage Kingston, she sensed, was even more that way than most . . . a full-grown wolf whose hunting instincts would make the seduction technique of bad Bobby Clay seem like a puppy's playful antics.

A man like Gage Kingston would go after a woman with heat and passion. He'd delight in the chase. He'd revel in the capture. *And*, she thought, before she could stop herself, *he'd make sure the woman reveled in it, as well*.

Resolutely Tara blocked the thought from going any further. She knew from sad experience that she didn't have the heat and passion a man like Gage would want in return; she didn't have the skill and insouciance to play what he undoubtedly thought of as a game; and, most of all, she didn't have the heart.

Which, even if she flat out told him, he'd never believe. Her outside was so sexy and spectacular that men never believed what was inside wasn't.

Men!

Even the most experienced of them seemed to lose a few brain cells when faced with anything larger than a B cup. Though, to be fair, she admitted, stealing a quick glance at him out of the corner of her eye, he seemed to be staring at her face and not at the swell of her breasts under the plain cotton blouse she was wearing. Still . . . did he *have* to ogle her like that?

She closed her book with a snap. "Do you mind?" she said, unable to bear his scrutiny another minute. Another second.

Gage lifted an eyebrow. "Mind?" he asked, still staring at her through his upraised fingers.

"I'm not some kind of exhibit."

"Ah, that's where you're wrong, Ms. Channing." He folded his index fingers down. "Dead wrong."

Tara's back stiffened. "You're saying I *am* an exhibit?"

"Not an exhibit," he corrected easily, smiling at her with all the unaffected charm of a Kingston born-and-bred. "An example. An exquisite example of ideal feminine beauty. The cinematographer in me is impressed. The man is . . ." he sighed and spread his hands with every bit of the unconscious theatrical grace his father or brother might have used ". . . awed by your magnificence."

Tara couldn't help it. She laughed. "The man is also full of bull," she countered, trying to make her burst of laughter sound like a snort of disgusted disbelief.

"I meant every word." Gage did his best to look wounded by her skepticism. "You are utterly magnificent and I am completely aw—"

She pursed her lips at him, her frown warning him against repeating such a ridiculous claim, but the unwilling twinkle in her eyes belied her stern expression.

His smile widened into a rogue's grin at the success of his ploy. He'd made her laugh, and women loved men who made them laugh. His mother had given her sons that priceless bit of information long ago, and experience had proved it to be true. "All right. Not awestruck," he conceded with a patently false and vastly appealing hint of sheepishness for having been caught exaggerating. "But close to it." *Uncomfortably close, if the truth be known.* "Would you believe, ah . . ." he cocked his head, as if thinking hard ". . . merely overwhelmed instead?"

Tara shook her head at him, trying to look both disapproving and bored. Judging by the satisfied look on his face, she was failing miserably.

"You scoff?" Gage asked, obviously warming to the chase.

"I scoff."

He laid a hand over his heart. "You wound me deeply."

"If you use that line very often, I'm surprised you haven't been 'wounded unto death' by now."

"Line?" he said with mock indignation. "You think I'm handing you a line?"

"I *know* you're handing me a line."

"You misjud—"

"Please." She held up a slender hand to stop him from speaking. This had to be nipped in the bud, she decided. Right now, and subtlety be damned. Any man who could make her laugh so easily, for such a lame reason, was even more dangerous than she'd first thought. "I've heard every line ever invented," she told him. "And every variation of every line. From the crude proposition of a construction worker on the street to the sophisticated versions you slick Hollywood types use, plus everything in between. I've heard *all* of them." She spoke the next three words slowly and precisely, for extra emphasis. "Every single one. And I want you to know, before this goes any further, that I'm not interested. It's nothing personal," she assured him. "I'm sure you're a very nice man. And I'm sure I'd probably have a very nice time if I *was* interested," she added, telling herself she'd said it as a sop to his male ego and not because it might actually be true. "That, however, is a moot point because I'm very definitely *not* interested. I'm very flattered, of course, but I'm not interested. Not at all. Not remotely. Not even a little bit. I *never* get involved with anyone I work with." She looked directly into his eyes, making sure he understood she was serious. "Never. Ever."

They looked at each other for a long second, both of them wary, waiting for what the other would say next.

Tara sat tensely, her chin up, her fingers tight around her book, wondering if she'd loused up her one chance to break out of the "other woman" roles she'd played for so long by being too blunt. But she was determined to be just as blunt again if need be. No acting job, no matter how good it was or how big a chance it offered, was worth getting her heart broken over. She'd walk off the set before she let that happen.

Gage stared back at her with a scowl on his face. The need to take her down a peg or two for the presumption inherent in her forthright little speech struggled against the sure and certain knowledge that giving in to a fit of masculine pique would only confirm what she so obviously thought of his motives. And, then, of course, he admitted wryly, there was the fact that she was correct in her presumption: he *had* been feeding her a line in an effort to arouse her interest. It'd been a sincere line, as lines went, but still a line. He decided to be magnanimous and forgive her. This time.

He smiled. "Never?" he asked, sounding remarkably like a small, hopeful boy inquiring about the possibility of another cookie.

"Never," Tara said firmly, refusing to let her lips curve even the slightest bit in response. *Nip it in the bud,* she reminded herself. If she let him charm her into smiling back at him now, there was no telling what he might try to charm her into—or out of—later. "Contrary to what you may have heard about me, I don't go in for location, ah . . . romances," she said, settling on the least distasteful word she could think of for the practice. "It just complicates the working rela—"

"Hey, there, gorgeous." A pair of large masculine hands settled on her shoulders from behind, and a masculine mouth nuzzled through her hair to plant a kiss on her ear.

Tara tilted her head back and smiled—a radiant, unrehearsed, unaffected, wholly welcoming smile. "Pierce," she exclaimed, turning her head so he could kiss her cheek. "What's up?"

"Hans has finished filling Jeremy in on a few pertinent facts of life and he wants us on our marks. Now."

"Already?" Tara glanced toward the set. "I didn't hear an explosion."

"I guess he was being gentle since the kid's so new an' all. But don't worry." Pierce's beautifully sculpted lips turned up in a grin of unholy anticipation. "If ol' Jere keeps acting up, Hans'll tear his head off."

"Pierce, please." Tara patted the hand on her shoulder. "I have no desire to see anyone's head torn off. Even someone as annoying as Jeremy Dean." She came to her feet as she spoke, turning slightly to drop her book onto the seat of her chair as she straightened. She was very careful not to look at Gage. "We'd better get back to work before Hans forgets all about Jeremy and takes a swipe at one of us for making him wait," she warned, starting toward the set.

"Hey." Pierce looped an arm around her shoulders to keep her from walking off ahead of him. "Stay next to me. Hans is too much of a gentleman to come after you." He pulled her close. "And he won't come after me if I'm with you."

Tara wrapped her arm around the tall actor's lean waist. "Don't worry, sweetie," she cooed, pulling him along beside her. "I won't let the big bad director hurt you."

She didn't see the teasing grin Pierce shot over her shoulder at his older brother. Nor the thunderstruck expression on Gage's face as he watched the two people the tabloids were already calling the "silver screen's hottest new couple" walk off toward the set with their heads together and their arms wrapped around each other.

Fury bubbled in Gage, hot and unexpectedly, shockingly intense. His eyes narrowed into slits. His hands clenched on the wooden arms of the chair as he fought not to give in to the unwelcome emotion.

"I never get involved with anyone I work with," she'd said, her voice serious and sincere, her big beautiful eyes as wide and guileless as a baby's. *"I don't go in for location romances,"* she'd said, looking as if butter wouldn't melt in her mouth.

He'd almost believed her. Almost swallowed that old chestnut whole. And then she'd smiled like a Christmas angel and snuggled up to Pierce like a ten-dollar hooker who'd just been offered her weight in diamonds for one night's work.

Just like Alyssa, he thought, fighting the urge to do something violent and stupid.

He wanted to stomp after them and yank her out of his brother's embrace and into his. He wanted to kiss her luscious mouth until she was mindless with a need and desire only he could satisfy. And then, damn it, he wanted her to smile at him the way she'd smiled at Pierce. Even if she didn't mean it.

"Hell," Gage said savagely, too low for anyone but himself to hear. The next thirty days or so—until Tara Channing wound up her stint on the movie and went back to her soap opera—were going to be goddamned long.

3

"DON'T LOOK NOW." Pierce whispered the words into the rippling cloud of Tara's hair as he drew her into a tender embrace. "But I think my big brother is a tad annoyed with us." The teasing note in his voice was totally at odds with the ardent expression on his face.

"Annoyed?" Tara whispered back, making it look as if she were moving her lips merely to nibble on Pierce's ear.

Slowly, looking as if he were savoring the anticipation, he began unbuttoning her blouse. "More like royally pissed off, actually." He murmured the words against her arched throat and dragged the open blouse down one shoulder to bare more of her satiny skin.

Tara curled her hands into his hair, pulling him to her breast, and bent her head over his. Her hair swung forward, obscuring both their faces. "Annoyed about what?" she demanded, as if she didn't already know all too well. As if she weren't already dreading the possible consequences of that annoyance.

"Don't try to kid a kidder," Pierce chided her as he slowly slid one hand from her waist to her thigh. "You know about what." He guided her backward toward the kitchen table as he spoke and gently lifted her onto it. "Gage isn't used to being turned down." The wicked chuckle of delight that rumbled through his chest as he bent over her looked like a shiver of uncontrollable passion. "I don't think he likes it."

"You don't have to sound so pleased about it," Tara hissed, turning her head into his bare chest so that her mouth would remain hidden from the cameras. It was an unnecessary precaution since film wasn't rolling yet, but Tara did it automatically. "And I didn't exactly turn him down. A man has to ask before he can—"

"Okay, that's enough," Hans called out. "Let's do it again. And can the chit-chat this time, will you?" he added, letting his stars know he was aware he hadn't had their full attention on the run-through. "We're going to roll film this time."

Tara hopped down off the table, pulling her blouse back into place and rebuttoning it as Makeup fussed with her hair and face. She smoothed the front of her skirt with both hands, making sure the blouse was tucked in, and then nodded at Hans, signaling her readiness to do the scene for real this time.

"Pierce?" Hans asked.

Pierce nodded.

"Quiet on the set," hollered the assistant director.

"Roll film," Hans ordered. "And . . . action."

They did it again, the tender embrace, the gentle fingers unbuttoning her blouse, the caressing slide of his palm down the side of her body. There were sighs and soft murmurs this time, and a heated kiss as Pierce lifted her onto the table.

"Cue Jeremy," Hans ordered softly as Pierce began to press Tara backward onto the table's smooth surface.

"*Yelena!*" Jeremy Dean, deeply immersed in his role as the post-communist revolutionary Yuri Zdravkovich, burst into the room. Snow, whipped up by a wind machine, swirled in behind him. "Whore!" he shouted, charging across the room to pull Pierce off his character's sister. "Traitorous whore!"

"Yuri, no!" Tara scrambled off the table as Pierce stumbled backward. "No!" she screamed, her eyes going wide with fear as she spied the gun in her make-believe brother's hand. She launched herself across the room, grabbing at his forearm with both hands. "Please, Yuri," she pleaded when he resisted her. "You cannot. Yuri, you cannot!"

He threw her off, sending her to the cold, hard linoleum of the kitchen floor with the force of his shove.

She was back on her feet instantly. "Please. I beg you. He is unarmed. You cannot shoot an unarmed man."

"Get out of the way, Yelena," Pierce ordered, softly and gently. The look on his face was cold and deadly. His lean body was poised and wary, his stance that of a man who was intimately familiar with all the more deadly forms of hand-to-hand combat.

"Yes, get out of the way, you treacherous bitch." Jeremy waved his gun in a way that was meant to be menacing but only served to show how unfamiliar he was with the deadly weapon. "This is a matter between men. I will deal with you after I have killed him."

"No! I will not let you." She grabbed at his gun arm. "I will—"

He threw her off again, landing what looked like a fierce backhanded slap to the side of her head. Tara cried out and fell against the wall, letting her head snap around as if propelled by the full force of his blow. She was utterly still for a moment and then she slowly lifted her head. Using one hand to push her heavy hair out of her eyes, she raised the other to her face, touching the back of it to her mouth as if to stanch the flow of blood.

Pierce roared with rage and launched himself at Jeremy.

A shot rang out.

"Nicolai!" Tara screamed.

A meticulously choreographed, carefully rehearsed fight ensued. The two men careened around the room in what looked like mortal combat, falling across the table where Yelena and Nicolai had so recently exchanged their passionate kisses, brushing dishes off the narrow kitchen counter, until, at last, they fell against the door together and crashed out into the snow.

"Cut!" hollered Hans, halting the action in mid-punch. "Good job, people." He looked over at Tara. "Are you all right, my dear?" he asked, referring to her crash into the wall.

Tara smiled and gave him a thumbs-up from her seat on the floor. "Piece of cake."

"Good. Then let's get set up for the reaction shots."

"Good God, that stuff's freezing," Pierce complained as he came back into the barn brushing snow off his bare arms and chest.

One of the crew members from Wardrobe handed him a towel. "Just be glad we're not really in Russia," she said, using another one to wipe snow off his back and the seat of his pants. "I hear it's at least, oh, a hundred-and-eighty degrees below zero there at this time of year."

"It isn't called Russia, anymore," Jeremy Dean informed them as he came in behind Pierce. "It's the Commonwealth of Independent States now. And we'd be in the state of Kazakhstan if we were *really* on location." He said it as if he was sorry they weren't.

Pierce shook his head. "Method actors," he muttered, too low for Jeremy to hear. The crew member giggled. Pierce winked at her. "I say if we're not really in...Kazakhstan, was it?" he asked Jeremy. The younger man nodded. "Well, if we're not really in Kazakhstan then we shouldn't have to use real snow, either. I mean, we're all professional actors here, right?"

"Yeah...right," Jeremy agreed with another nod.

"Then why can't we just *act* like we're freezing our butts off? Yo, Hans," he hollered at the director. "Jere and I think we shouldn't have to use real snow on this next take. How 'bout getting the Special Effects guys to rig something up so that—"

"After you're dried off and prettied up I want Nicolai's reaction when he sees the gun," Hans said, ignoring Pierce's nonsense. "And then again when Yuri hits Yelena." He turned to his A.D. "Have somebody get Miss Channing a blood capsule," he ordered. "I want a close up of her face after he hits her."

"I'll stay right here, then," Tara said, sinking back down to the floor. If she got up, she'd just have to get back down in a couple of minutes. And the floor wasn't all that cold now that the door was closed again. Still, she looked up with an appreciative smile when someone draped a jacket over her shoulders. Her expression only faltered a little bit when she saw who that someone was.

"You okay?" Gage inquired, crouching down beside her.

"I'm fine," she said, surprised he'd even bother to ask. In her experience, a spurned man wasn't normally considerate of the woman who had done the spurning.

"You hit the wall pretty hard."

"Not all that hard." She shrugged lightly and then winced at the twinge in her shoulder.

"Damn it, you're *not* okay."

"I'm fine," she insisted, resisting the urge to rub at her upper arm. "The landing was just a little rougher than I expected it to be, is all," she assured him. "It's nothing."

"Jeremy shoved you harder than you expected him to is what you mean," he growled, amazed at the surge of anger he felt at the thought of anyone hurting her.

"Really, I'm fine." Tara reached out, putting her hand on his forearm to stop him from rising to his feet. She wasn't sure what prompted her to do it except that he suddenly looked more than a little dangerous. "I'm fine, Gage."

He glowered at her, clearly unconvinced.

"All that happened was that I got carried away and hit the wall a little harder than I intended to," she said, with a self-deprecating smile meant to downplay the situation and defuse whatever it was that was making him look so fierce. "But it's no big deal. And it certainly wasn't anyone's fault. It doesn't even hurt anymore." She rolled her shoulder to prove it. "See?"

He continued to glower.

"Gage?" She squeezed his arm. "It wasn't anyone's fault," she repeated, looking up at him to make sure he agreed. "Okay?"

Their gazes caught. And held. And kept holding. It was suddenly as if there were no one else in the big barn but the two of them. No one else in the world. He forgot to be suspicious. She forgot to be wary. They both forgot all the reasons they shouldn't . . . *couldn't* . . . get involved with one another.

"Okay?" Tara repeated softly. Her voice was little more than a husky whisper. Her eyes were wide and a bit dazed. Her lips were moist and slightly parted, as if in invitation.

"Okay," he agreed, although he couldn't have said, just then, what he was agreeing to. But, hell, as long as she looked at him like that, he'd agree to anything. *Everything.* "Tara," he murmured, lifting his hand to her cheek.

"Miss Channing? Ah, Miss Channing? Here's your blood capsule."

Gage dropped his hand.

Tara slowly shifted her gaze. "Yes? Oh...thank you," she said to the young man, letting go of Gage's arm to take the offered capsule. "It's Arlo, isn't it?" she asked, still looking up at him.

The young man blushed. "Yes, ma'am."

"Well, thank you, Arlo. I appreciate it."

"Oh, it's no trouble, Miss Channing. Anytime." He backed away as he spoke, nearly stumbling over his own feet but apparently unable to look away from her long enough to watch where he was going. "That's what

I'm here for. To help. If you need anything—anything at all—you just let me know."

Her smile of thanks widened into one of sincere pleasure. "Thank you. I will."

"And another one bites the dust," Gage muttered.

Still smiling, Tara turned her gaze on him. "I beg your pardon?"

"Just how many men do you have to have panting after you to make you happy? Not," he added, before she could answer him, "that that one's a man yet."

Tara's smile faded and her eyes went ice-cold. "I like them young," she said. "And in droves. Or hadn't you heard?" She made a move as if to get up.

"No, stay there, dear," Hans said, waving her down as he approached. "You're perfect right where you are. Do you have your blood capsule?"

Tara showed it to him.

"Good. Good. We're all set, then." He glanced over at Gage as if he'd only just seen him. "Aren't you on the wrong side of the camera? Again?"

"He was just leaving," Tara responded for him, her tone as frigid as the look in her eyes.

Gage hesitated for a moment, crouched there beside her on the balls of his feet, his forearms balanced on his knees, looking as if he might say something.

"Weren't you?" Tara goaded.

He surged to his feet and stalked off without a word.

Hans raised one grizzled eyebrow. "Is there something going on here I should know about?" he asked Tara.

"Not a thing," she said blithely, hiding her hurt feelings and anger behind a careless smile and a too-bright manner.

Hans sighed and hunkered down in front of her, reaching out to take one of her hands in his. "I'm an old man, my dear—"

"Distinguished," Tara corrected, giving him a coquettish look out of the corners of her eyes. It didn't quite cover the painful emotions she was trying to conceal.

"Old," Hans insisted, shaking his head at her. "And experienced. Which enables me to see that this charming little performance is more for his benefit—" he tilted his head toward Gage "—than mine." He sighed again. "I wasn't even aware the two of you were involved."

Tara jerked her hand out of his. "We're not involved," she said vehemently. "We barely know each other."

"Ah." Hans nodded. "So that's it. He's hot on your trail and you haven't decided whether you're going to let him catch you or not. I should've known it was something like that after that scene on the bed yesterday."

"Hans!" She glanced around quickly, afraid someone might overhear their conversation. "It's nothing like that."

"So you say, but does Gage feel the same way?"

"I haven't got the least idea how Gage feels. Nor do I care," she lied. "And—" she lifted her chin in a delicately disdainful gesture "—I hardly think it's any of your business, anyway."

"Anything that affects this movie is my business, my dear. You'd do well to keep that in mind."

"Is that some kind of a threat, Hans?"

"No, my dear, not a threat. Merely a friendly warning. The same warning Gage is going to get—"

"You wouldn't!"

"I would—if the situation between you starts to interfere with my movie."

"It won't," Tara assured him, hoping it was true. "*Nothing* is going to interfere with this movie."

"Good. That's good." He patted her shoulder, then pushed himself to his feet. "Put that capsule in your mouth, then, and let's get this scene in the can."

WHATEVER HANS HAD SAID to her about her motivation for the scene, Gage thought, it had been exactly the right thing. She began it huddled over, her slender shoulders hunched, her hair fanned out over the floor as if she'd just fallen beneath the force of Jeremy's backhanded blow.

"And . . . action," Hans directed.

She pushed herself up slowly, her hands braced against the linoleum floor, her unbuttoned blouse hanging open. The plain cotton bra beneath it shouldn't have been the least bit enticing, but was. She hung there for a second or two, as if dazed, her head still down, her face obscured by the heavy fall of her hair. And then she lifted her head, and one slender hand came up to shove her hair out of her eyes. She looked directly into the camera.

For just a moment, her wide-eyed gaze was full of astonishment and pain and a sort of bewildered betrayal—as if she could scarcely believe her brother had actually struck her. She straightened, squaring her frail shoulders, and raised her other hand to her mouth, touching the back of it to the blood that trickled down her chin. The look of hurt astonishment gave way to one of deep anger. With just a lift of her chin and a slight narrowing of her eyes, she silently conveyed her contempt for the man who had hit her, as well as a reckless defiance that seemed to dare him to do it again.

Behind his camera, Gage had the uncomfortable feeling that the anger and scorn coming at him through his lens wasn't entirely manufactured. Nor entirely meant for the fictional Yuri. Honesty—and a nagging sense of guilt—compelled him to admit that it wasn't entirely undeserved, either.

Face it, Kingston. Even if it was God's own truth, what you said to her was petty and mean. Not to mention way out of line. You were lucky she didn't slap your face.

"Give me an extreme close-up of her mouth," Hans instructed in an undertone.

Automatically Gage zoomed in until her bloodied lips filled up his monitor. They looked incredibly soft and vulnerable, their slight, almost infinitesimal trembling betraying the deep hurt her defiant eyes tried to deny.

Gage felt like a heel, like a monster who tore the wings off defenseless butterflies, like a beast who kicked puppies, like an unenlightened chauvinist boar who'd been deliberately cruel to a defenseless, utterly blameless woman.

He owed her an apology, he realized, staring transfixed at those quivering lips. An abject, groveling apology, delivered on his knees, if that's what it took for her to forgive him. He wondered how far away the nearest florist was. Or if it was possible to get chocolates delivered in the wilds of Montana in the middle of winter.

"Cut! And print!"

LOOKING NEITHER to the right or left, Tara grabbed her book and hurried to her trailer when her scene was over knowing that Hans wouldn't need her for the rest of the afternoon.

Her trailer was small but luxuriously appointed, with everything she'd need even if she didn't come out for the next two weeks. And it had a lock. Right now, she needed the security of being able to turn a lock against the world.

One member of the world in particular.

Why do men have to be so ... so darned predictable? So darned judgmental? She threw her book against the wall above the white leather sofa and watched it bounce harmlessly to the floor. *So darned male!*

Almost every man she had ever met had expected her to live up to some impossible image he had of her, to conform to some preconceived notion he carried in his head that had nothing to do with who she really was. It was something she'd learned to live with. To expect. So why was she so hurt and angry over the fact that Gage Kingston was acting like every other man in the world?

She picked up her tape player from the low cocktail table and heaved it against the wall after her book. It landed with a satisfying crash and broke in two, spilling its plastic guts onto the sofa and ejecting a cassette into the air. Tara had to duck to keep it from hitting her in the head.

"Smart move," she muttered, feeling like a fool. She never lost her temper. Never had tantrums. Never went on crying jags.

So why was she throwing things?

And why did she feel like stomping her feet and screaming at the top of her lungs?

And why were hot, unwelcome tears burning at the backs of her eyes?

"Stress," she said out loud, trying very hard to believe it. "Just stress and nerves."

Her role as the doomed Yelena Zdravkovich could be the break she'd been waiting for. It didn't matter that the role was a relatively small one, or that Yelena would be killed by one of her brother's cohorts before the movie was half over.

What mattered was that the role was meaty and important, light-years removed from every brainless bimbo and faithless "other woman" role she'd ever played.

What mattered was that she had been second choice, a last minute replacement after the actress who'd originally been signed for the part had unexpectedly announced she would be spending the next few months at the Betty Ford Clinic.

What mattered was that the part had been given to her by the Kingstons and could be taken away just as easily. She'd only put in two days' filming so far, just two small scenes among the handful she had. If she wasn't careful, she could be replaced easier than the film in Gage's camera.

It was no wonder she felt stressed out, she told herself. No wonder she was concerned and nervous about the opinion of anyone who wielded any power at all over the outcome of the film, let alone someone who wielded as much power as a Kingston did. Seen in that light, her screaming nerves and shaky emotional state were completely understandable. They had nothing— *absolutely nothing*—to do with her acute disappointment that Gage Kingston was just as boorish and predatory as any other man on the make.

Tara sighed, knowing she was committing the unpardonable sin of lying to herself. At this stage in her life she could handle the ordinary man on the make with one hand tied behind her back. What she was having trouble with was her own nascent desire to respond with a great deal more than cool disdain and amused detachment to this distinctly unordinary predatory male. She sighed again, knowing there was only one antidote to what ailed her. And throwing things wasn't it.

Heading into the tiny bedroom of the trailer, she shed Yelena's plain cotton blouse. Stepping out of the wool skirt, thick stockings and sturdy, unattractive shoes her character wore, she exchanged them for a set of bright purple sweats and a pair of well-worn sneakers. She creamed off her makeup and the fake blood, fastened her hair into a high ponytail and went back into the living area to climb onto her exercise bike.

Ten hard, fast miles and her nerves would begin to settle down. Twenty miles and she might be able to face Gage Kingston without wanting to slap him silly. Or burst into tears. Or both. Twenty-five miles and she might even be able to figure out how to hold him off without riling him up—or exposing her own terrifying attraction to him in the process. And if that didn't do it, she could always try to wear herself out with the free weights.

The odometer on the stationary bike had just turned on the eighteenth mile when someone knocked on her trailer door. Tara ignored it, hoping whoever it was would go away.

"Come on, Tara, open the door," Gage said. "I know you're in there."

Oh, no, Tara thought, pedaling faster. *Not now. Not yet.*

She hadn't formulated any sort of strategy yet, didn't have a clue as to how she was going to deal with him now that he'd made it clear that her I-never-get-involved-with-anyone-I-work-with routine, honest though it was, wasn't going to be enough to deter him. She'd thought she'd have at least until tomorrow morning to regroup and plan before she had to face him again. Obviously Gage Kingston was too impatient to wait until she emerged from her trailer on her own.

There was another knock, harder than the last one. "Tara? Open the door." He paused. "Please."

Tara sighed and stopped pedaling. Much as she wanted to, she couldn't leave a Kingston standing out in the snow. Especially when he'd said please. She got off the exercise bike, picked up a towel and crossed the narrow trailer to the door, hurriedly formulating a plan as she did so.

Okay, she thought, taking several deep breaths before she flipped open the lock, *this is it.* If he expected sophisticated and cynical, well, then, she'd give him sophisticated and cynical. In spades. She opened the door.

"Yes?" she asked, dabbing at her face with the fluffy peach towel so she could avoid having to look at him. "What is it?"

"I'd like to talk to you for a minute."

"Shouldn't you be behind a camera somewhere?"

"We're finished for the day," he told her. "And I'd like to talk to you."

Tara propped a shoulder against the doorframe. "So talk."

"May I come inside?" Gage asked politely, reminding himself that he was here to apologize to her. He wasn't going to jump her luscious bones, no matter how hot and tousled and tempting she looked. And he wasn't going to let himself get irritated by her snooty ice-queen attitude. He was going to say his piece and leave, and that would be that. Because that was all it could be. All he would let it be. He smiled, trying to appear harmless and contrite. "It's freezing out here," he complained.

Tara shrugged as if it didn't matter to her one way or the other what he did. "It isn't going to be any warmer in here, if that's what you're thinking, but suit yourself." She turned away from the door, moving into the tiny peach-and-white kitchenette as he stepped up into the trailer. "I'm going to have some juice," she said, as the door banged shut behind him. "Would you like some?"

"No, thanks," he said, admiring the fluid, feline sway of her hips as she walked away from him. He couldn't help but wonder if she'd move that well when she was flat on her back under a man. *Under me*, he amended and then immediately squelched the wayward thought. He wasn't into torturing himself with images of something he'd already decided he couldn't have.

"Wine?" she offered over her shoulder. "I think there's some Chardonnay in here."

"No, no wine."

"You're out of luck if you want beer. There isn't any."

"I don't want any beer, either. Tara—"

She turned around with a large glass of grapefruit juice in her hand, and leaned back against the counter. "What?" she asked, her eyes distant and chilly as she stared at him over the rim of the glass.

Gage ran a hand through his hair, unsure where to start. It was an uncomfortable feeling, made more so by the way she lounged against the counter, obviously waiting for him to say whatever he had come to say and leave. "Look, Tara, I—" He wasn't used to having a woman look at him in such a coolly disparaging way, as if she'd weighed him and found him wanting. He didn't like it. He also didn't like the hint of amusement in her eyes, as if she were enjoying watching him squirm. "You're not going to make this easy for me, are you?"

"Make what easy for you?"

"Damn it, Tara, I'm trying to apologize here."

"Really?" She took a sip of her juice to hide her surprise. "For what?"

Gage frowned at her. What did she mean, *For what?* What had that fierce anger been all about? That look of stunned betrayal she'd sent him through the lens of his camera? That lip quivering that had made him feel like such a heel? Had it all just been acting, after all? Had he been taken in—again? "For that crack I made about Arlo," he clarified, on the off chance that she hadn't been just acting. "It was completely uncalled for."

Tara took another quick sip of juice. "Oh, that." She dismissed it with a lift of her shoulder, as if the insult had been less than nothing to her; as if his apology were less than nothing, too. The truth was, it sent a warm glow all through her; she couldn't remember the last time a man had apologized for misjudging her. "Well—" she gestured at him with her glass "—go ahead and apologize, if it will make you feel better, but it's not going to change anything," she said, hoping he couldn't see it for the lie it was. Hoping, too, that she wasn't overdoing the sophisticated-and-cynical bit. "Between you and me, I mean."

"I don't expect it to."

Tara arched an eyebrow. "Don't you?"

"Hell, no—all right, yes, damn it. I do," he said, forgetting that it couldn't.

Her lips curved in a derisive little smile. "Don't count on it."

"God, you're a hard one, aren't you?" he said, but even as the words escaped from his mouth, he wasn't convinced they were entirely true. Or entirely false, either. Damn it, how the hell was a man supposed to know when an actress was acting and when she wasn't? And why in hell did he care, anyway? He ran a hand through his hair again. "I think I'll take that glass of Chardonnay, after all," he said, just to give himself some time to think.

Tara put her grapefruit juice down on the counter. "Fine." She turned toward the refrigerator to get it for him.

As she found a glass and poured the wine, she struggled with the urge to do the polite thing and offer him a seat. It was what her mother would have done. *But I'm not my mother*, she reminded herself. Her aim wasn't to impress him with her lovely Southern manners and her feminine wiles but to help him realize that he didn't really want her, after all.

Which, she decided, catching sight of her reflection in the shiny black glass door of the microwave, might not be as hard as she'd thought it would be. Even before she'd left Texas all those years ago, she'd learned that most men preferred not to deal with the imperfect reality of a flesh and blood woman. And, at the moment, she was about as real as it got—an unmade-up, scraggly haired, out-of-breath, sweaty female couldn't possibly have been what Gage Kingston had had in mind when he came pounding on her trailer door. Added to her condescending bitch act, her present state of dishevelment just might be enough to make him wonder what he ever saw in her.

She turned back to him with the glass of wine in her hand and a cool smile on her lips, prepared to make another well-chilled and faintly amused comment—

nothing deflated a man's . . . ego faster than the suspicion that the woman he wanted might be laughing at him—only to see him standing beside the sofa, staring down at the tapeplayer parts strewn across the soft white leather.

"Have a little accident?" he asked, looking up as she approached him with the wineglass held out in front of her. There was a satisfied look on his face, as if he'd just discovered something that pleased him.

"I dropped it."

Gage quirked an eyebrow and glanced at the tapeplayer-size indentation in the trailer wall. A teasing little grin lifted one side of his mouth. "Dropped?"

Tara could feel her cheeks heating. "Here's your wine," she said stiffly, setting the glass down on the coffee table with a sharp click.

Gage's grin widened. "Is that a polite way of telling me to mind my own business?"

"Yes." The word was as frosty as the first snowfall of winter, but her cheeks were the color of hothouse roses.

The temptation to make those roses bloom even more proved irresistible. "Temper, temper," Gage chided, immeasurably heartened by the knowledge that she wasn't nearly as cool and controlled as she pretended. There was real fire under that icy, unconcerned facade, after all. A real woman inside the actress. Under Alyssa's beautiful exterior, there hadn't been anything but cunning and control. "Were you pretending you were aiming at my head, by any chance?"

Tara turned away from him without answering, intent on escaping to the relative safety of the tiny kitchenette.

He reached out and grabbed her arm, just above the elbow. "Don't go."

She went as stiff as a poker. "Let go of me."

"Tara, I just want—"

"I know what you want," Tara interrupted. "And I want you to let go of me."

"Will you promise not to run away again?"

"I wasn't running away. I was going to get my juice." She looked down at the hand that held her prisoner. It was undeniably a man's hand, large and tanned, with a sprinkling of fine dark hairs on the back of it. Strong and gentle, in that indefinable way that only a man's hand can be, holding her fast without hurting her. The thumb and fingers were long enough to overlap where they curled around the soft flesh of her upper arm, and if he moved them, even just a little, they'd brush against the outer curve of her left breast.

Tara pressed her lips together to keep from asking him to do just that. She hadn't been touched intimately, except in front of a camera, for nearly five years, and she suddenly wanted very much to be touched. By him. Her nipples budded against the fabric of her purple sweatshirt, unashamed to ask for what she wouldn't.

"Do you mind?" she managed finally, horrified by her body's betrayal. "I asked you to let me go."

Gage did so reluctantly. She looked faint and fragile all of the sudden, as if she were about to go into what his mother would have termed a swoon. "Sit down," he said, bending to brush the broken tape player into the far corner of the sofa. "I'll get your juice." He pressed her down onto the white leather. "You sit down."

Unable to do anything else, Tara sat.

Gage hurried into the kitchenette to grab her juice off the counter. "Here you are," he said, holding it out to her. When she didn't take it, he put it on the coffee table next to his wine and sat down beside her. "Are you feeling dizzy? Faint? Do you need a doctor?"

"No, I—" Her mind was all hazy and she couldn't quite catch her breath. She closed her eyes, trying to think.

"Tara?" He touched her arm again.

She jerked away and opened her eyes. "I'm just a little, um . . . a little light-headed," she lied. Never in a million years would she admit that it had been pure, unadulterated, giddy lust causing her to go all woozy and weak-kneed. "From the bike," she explained, gesturing vaguely toward the exercise equipment in the corner of the trailer. "I usually do a long cool-down routine before I stop." She reached for her grapefruit juice, holding it carefully in both hands to keep from spilling it. "And I didn't do it this time. The blood must have rushed from my head or something." She took a sip of the juice, then another, praying that the craving to have him put his hands all over her naked flesh would go away as quickly as it had come. "Whatever it was, it's gone," she lied again. "I'm fine now."

"You don't look fine," he said, staring into her face. Her skin was flushed, her breathing uneven, her eyes vague and kind of dazed looking. It could have been caused by the sudden cessation of exercise but . . . *I'll be damned if she doesn't look like a woman in the throes,* he thought. If he'd had her buck naked and spread-eagled under him, he would have sworn she was on the verge of a rip-roaring climax.

But that was crazy, he told himself. Wasn't it?

She was flushed because she was angry and embarrassed about losing her temper. She was panting because she'd just gotten off an exercise bike. And her eyes were . . .

Oh, those eyes of hers, he thought, staring into them, *those wide, hypnotic, mesmerizing, soul-stealing eyes of hers.*

They were soft and warm; luminous with sensual longing, hazy with the sweet ache of unfulfilled desire. They were the eyes of a woman both bedazzled and dazzling, and they were wreaking havoc on his good intentions, making him forget that he'd come knocking on her trailer door just to apologize. Making him forget to be on his guard. Making him forget that Pierce appeared to have first claim on her affections. Making him forget . . . everything. Except the one thing that nothing in the world could make him forget.

He wanted her.

Desperately.

And, from all the outward signs, he could swear that she wanted him, too.

If she didn't, if she was already committed to Pierce—or anyone else, for that matter—she could damn well speak up. He reached out, taking her glass of juice away from her to set it back on the coffee table.

She continued to stare at him, wide-eyed and breathless but making no move to stop him.

He put his hands on her shoulders.

She didn't say a word. Didn't move a muscle.

He pulled her to him and, very slowly, lowered his mouth to within millimeters of hers.

Her hands clenched into fists at her sides. Her eyes closed. Her head fell back.

"Tara?" His warm breath brushed against her lips, teasing her with the promise of his kiss, asking her if she wanted it as much as he did.

"Yes," she said fiercely, reaching up to curl her fingers in his hair. "God help me, *yes!*"

4

His mouth came down on hers with passionate voracity. There was no gentle tasting or teasing, no preliminary nibbling of her lips or tentative forays with the tip of his tongue. No subtlety. No technique. No finesse. Just searing heat and a driving, mindless hunger to possess. He pushed his tongue between her parted lips and wrapped his arms around her, pressing her down into the soft white leather of the sofa with the weight of his body. He slipped his knee between her thighs to make a place for himself, pressing his pelvis against her feminine mound.

Tara responded wildly, clinging to him as he tipped her backward, holding on as if he were the only solid thing in a world suddenly gone all topsy-turvy. Her fingers grasped his hair to pull him closer. Her mouth opened wider to receive his plundering tongue. Her thighs softened, spreading to accommodate him as he moved against her. She felt helpless and overwhelmed, as if she were being swept along in a sensual whirlpool; as if, like the proverbial moth to a flame, she were being inexorably drawn toward the inevitable consummation of a heated, heedless passion with no time for second thoughts or caution. It frightened her and excited her and made her forget, for a long, delicious moment, that the cost of loving was far too high.

And then Gage worked his hand under the damp purple fleece of her sweatshirt and cupped the fullness of her bare breast in his palm. Heat seared through her and she cried out, her body going utterly still as hard reality came crashing back in on her.

Oh, my God, what am I doing?

Suddenly frantic, she untangled her fingers from his hair and placed her hands against his shoulders to push him away. "Gage," she whispered, pressing her head back into the cushions to escape his kiss. "Gage, please."

"Yes," he murmured against her lips. "I'll please you. Anything you want." He dragged his open mouth down the arched column of her throat with fevered haste. "Any way you want it. Just tell me."

She could feel him levering himself to his elbows over her, tugging at the hem of her sweatshirt, pushing it up out of the way as he moved his head down the front of her body. She stiffened in anticipation and longing and dread. Oh, how she wanted what he was about to do! She wanted it with an intensity that frightened her, wanted it so badly that it was all she could do not to take his face in her hands and guide his hot, greedy mouth to her aching nipple.

She almost did it. Almost gave in to the unreasoning need that had her trembling beneath him. She even put her hands on his cheeks but, in the end, it was only to hold him away from her breasts.

"Gage," she moaned, fully aware that she was fighting her own desire, as well as his. "Gage, stop."

He pushed blindly against her hands, his mouth open and seeking, his own hands cupping and lifting her breasts to bring them closer. His tongue brushed her rigid nipple.

Tara whimpered in pleasure and mounting fear. It felt so good, so very good, but it made her vulnerable in ways she couldn't afford to be vulnerable. She'd forgotten all about protecting her part as Yelena; it was her heart she was protecting now.

"Gage, please. You've got to stop. Right now," she gasped, afraid she couldn't keep saying no if he didn't do what she asked in the very next second. *"Stop. Please."*

Something in her voice finally got through to him. He lifted his head. "Stop? You want me to stop?" His hot amber eyes were full of incredulity and frustrated male passion. His lower body was still pressed intimately against hers. His hands still cupped her breasts. *"Now?"*

"Yes." She slid her hands down from either side of his face to push against his shoulders again.

He didn't budge an inch. "Why?"

"Because I don't—" She turned her head away, unable to bear his fierce, unbelieving scrutiny. "Because I'm not—"

A dim light went on in his passion-fogged brain. "Don't worry. I have protection," he assured her.

"No, it isn't that." It should have been, she realized, but it wasn't. She hadn't even *thought* about protection. "It's just—that is, I don't—"

"Don't what?"

Don't want you, was what she wanted to say— should have said—but she couldn't make herself give voice to such a blatant lie. Because the truth was she wanted him too much, with a hunger she hadn't felt since she was seventeen years old and in love for the first time. And that wanting made her afraid. Afraid of him and what he made her feel. Afraid of disappointing him. Of being disappointed herself. Of letting herself be vulnerable. Of getting hurt.

"So you're involved with my brother, after all," Gage said, the words a ragged whisper against her averted cheek. Damn it, he'd known she was Pierce's! But she was so hot—she'd gotten *him* so hot—he'd let himself be fooled into thinking he'd misread the signs. No woman could respond so completely, so wildly to one man when she was already bound to another unless . . .

He looked down at her, at the artfully trembling lips and the faint gleam of tears not quite hidden beneath the demurely lowered lashes. His mouth twisted in derision and disgust.

. . .unless the woman was an actress looking for fame and fortune. Then she was capable of anything.

Furious—at her, at himself—Gage took Tara's chin in his fingers and turned her face to his. "Look at me," he demanded tightening his fingers when her lids remained lowered. "Damn it, Tara, look at me."

Slowly, afraid he would see the need still simmering inside her, afraid he could make her surrender to that need with the sheer force of his own, she lifted her gaze to his. Her expression was full of wariness and confusion, overlaid with the sweet ache of thwarted desire.

His face was as hard and unyielding as stone.

"Are you sleeping with Pierce?"

She stared at him for a second more, her slanted aquamarine eyes wide and uncomprehending, her mouth soft and vulnerable. And then fury ripped what he said became clear, fury ripped through her, completely replacing the passion of a moment before.

"You bastard!" she hissed. "You evil-minded bastard! Get off me!" She reared up, pushing at his shoulders with her hands, scrambling backward on the sofa to get out from under him as quickly as possible. "Just get off me!" she demanded fiercely, yanking down her sweatshirt as she struggled to her feet beside the sofa.

Gage got to his feet, too, and stood staring down at her with that hard, implacable look still on his face. There were going to be no more assumptions, he decided. No more guessing or speculating on the exact status of her relationship with Pierce. She was going to say it straight and put him out of his misery. "Is that a yes or no?"

"How *dare* you!" Her voice was low, furious and lethal. Her eyes were dark and narrowed, shooting sparks of rage. Her palms itched to slap him. "How dare you accuse me of something like that! As if I would be here with you, like this, as if I would let you climb all over me, or even kiss me if I were . . . if Pierce and I were . . ." Words failed her.

"Yes or no?"

"I don't owe you an answer to that." She lifted her chin. "I *won't* answer that."

"Tara—"

"You're the one who came sniffing around me like some kind of animal in rut," she reminded him, feelings of outrage making her forget the need to tread cautiously. "I didn't go looking for you. *You*—" she jabbed a finger against his chest "—came knocking on *my* door. Remember that when you start wondering if someone's betraying your precious brother."

"Damn it, Tara." He grabbed her hand and yanked her closer. So close that she could see the little gold flecks in his amber eyes. So close that she could feel his breath on her face as he spoke each low, fierce word. "I want a straight answer. Are you sleeping with Pierce?"

Tara stood her ground, refusing to cower or back down. "What's between Pierce and me is none of your business," she said, trying to jerk her hand out of his.

He transferred his grip to her shoulders and held her fast. "After what happened on that couch, it is. Because I refuse to cuckold my own brother." He shook her once. Hard. *"Are you sleeping with Pierce?"*

"Pierce and I are friends!" Tara all but shouted the words at him. "That's all, friends! Is that so hard to believe? That a man and a woman could just be friends? Nonsexual, platonic friends?"

"Not a woman like you," he replied, stunned by the sense of relief that rushed through him at her words, yet afraid to let himself truly believe them. If she was lying . . . if she was playing another part . . . *like Alyssa.* He shook his head, slowly, as if to clear it.

"Oh, that's right, I forgot," Tara said sarcastically, reading his movement as further negation of her words. She wrenched her shoulders, trying and failing to twist out of his grasp. "According to you and the tabloids, women like me don't have friends, do we? Especially men friends. We make conquests. We take lovers. We *break up* friendships, but we don't *have* them. We're too selfish and spoiled for that. Too sex-crazed. Too grasping. Too con—"

"Too beautiful. Too sexy. Too seductive," Gage corrected her softly, inflamed and aroused all over again by her passionate anger, and her equally passionate denial. Could a woman this angry lie? And did he really care? "Too damned tempting for any man to resist."

"Well, try!" she ordered, twisting her shoulders again, to no avail. She lifted her hands to his chest and pushed, trying to arch her body away from him. "And let go of me!"

"I can't."

"You mean you won't," Tara accused, made even more furious by her inability to get free. "And do you know why? Because you're just like all men on the make—as spoiled and amoral and oversexed as you'd like to believe I am, so you can tell yourself it wasn't your fault because I led you on. Men like you betray friendships and brothers and cheat on their wives and when you get caught all you can say is, *she tempted me*, as if that absolves you of all wrongdoing. Well, I've got news for you, Mr. High-and-Mighty Kingston, it doesn't. Men have been using that tired old line since Adam blamed Eve for the fall. It wasn't true then and it isn't true now." She stopped, flushed and out of breath, and glared up at him, as if daring him to refute a word she'd said.

He smiled at her. "Are you sleeping with anyone else?" The query was casual, almost offhand, as if it were merely some minor point he wanted to clear up.

"No, I'm not! Not that that's any of your business, either." *The nerve of the man! The absolute colossal nerve!* "Now let me go."

Gage shook his head. "Oh, no," he said softly, his smile becoming very male. Very satisfied. And very, very predatory. He much preferred this flaming virago to the cool sophisticate who'd greeted him at the door. She was more real. More natural and uncalculated. A woman couldn't act, couldn't lie, he decided, when she was mad enough to spit. "I can't let you go. Not now. Not yet." He tightened his hands on her shoulders, gently but inescapably, and drew her even closer.

"Gage!" She squirmed in his hold, turning her head to avoid his descending lips. "Weren't you listening to a word I said?"

He took her face in his hand to hold her still. "Only the important ones," he murmured just before his lips took hers.

Tara stood stock-still, her fingers curled, motionless, against his chest, unable to believe he was actually kissing her. Now, after all she'd just said to him, after the vile accusation he'd made, he thought he could just kiss her and make it all better. That was another male tactic as old as Adam—kissing an angry woman to turn her up sweet. *Men!* They thought the whole world ran on hormones. Well, it wasn't going to work. He could kiss her until "I Love Lucy" went out of syndication in every country in the world and it wouldn't change a thing. Not a thing. *Let's just see how he likes kissing a frozen stump,* she thought, resolving to stand absolutely still, to remain absolutely unresponsive for as long as it took him to realize that she wasn't kissing him back.

It didn't take long.

He eased his lips from hers just enough to speak. "Is this a challenge?" he asked softly.

Tara stared straight through him, her hands flat on his chest, her mouth screwed up like a child refusing a spoonful of bitter medicine.

She felt him smile against her lips. "You should probably know I can't resist a challenge any more than I seem to be able to resist you," he informed her. He slid his hands up to either side of her head as he spoke, cradling it, tilting it back for better access, and pressed his mouth down on hers again.

His kiss was different this time. Softer. Sweeter. Warm instead of hot. Moist instead of wet. He was asking for a response instead of demanding one. Coaxing instead of insisting. Feasting instead of gorging. His lips plucked lazily at her unresponsive mouth, brushing back and forth across it with his, sucking lightly at her closed lips. He licked at the seam between them with teasing strokes of his tongue, urging her to return the caress.

Tara stood stiffly, locking her limbs against the trembling that had seized them, refusing to open her mouth, refusing to thaw, refusing to give in to the riot of warm, melting feelings his kiss was evoking inside her.

With a sigh and a last slow flick of his tongue across her tightly closed lips, Gage abandoned her mouth to lay siege to less well fortified territory. He angled her head farther back, holding its weight in his palms, and took his lips on a slow journey across the sculpted bones of her face. He kissed his way up her jaw to the delicate skin of her temples and across the lids of her eyes, closing them in the process. He kissed her finely arched eyebrows and her smooth forehead. He nuzzled her nose with his, breathing her in as if she were perfume, and rubbed his stubbled cheek against hers, softly, letting her feel the contrast between them. And then, finally, he heard her breath catch in her throat and felt her hands flex ever so slightly against his chest, he wrapped his arms around her and brought his mouth back to hers.

"I'm sorry," Gage murmured against her lips. "For what I said about Arlo. And for what I implied about Pierce. I'm truly sorry."

Tara made a strangled noise of disagreement behind her closed lips, afraid to open them for fear he'd take advantage of it but completely powerless to turn away from his sweet, mind-drugging kisses, either.

"All right," he agreed, reading her objection correctly, despite the mangled form of communication. "Maybe I did more than imply." He spoke the soft words between the equally soft kisses he continued to press against her mouth. "But I had to know. I want you very badly," he stated baldly. "And my judgment's a little skewed because of it. All right," he amended, when her disagreement rumbled against his lips again. "A lot skewed. I haven't been thinking straight since yesterday morning when you looked at me through the lens of my camera like you wanted to eat me up, and then made love to Pierce."

"I wasn't looking at you," she muttered, stung into defending herself. "And I wasn't making love to Pierce. I was acting."

"I know. But I was jealous, anyway," he admitted, amazed that it was so. "Pea green with jealousy, without any right to be. But I want that right." He plucked at her lips with his, teasing her with his heat, teasing himself with the knowledge that she was very close to surrendering everything to him. He could feel it in the way her lips had softened against his; in the way her body leaned into his embrace instead of straining against it; in the way her hands rested against his chest. "Will you give me the right to be jealous of you? At least for a while?"

"Why should I?" Tara murmured.

"Because you want me, too?" he suggested.

"No, I don—"

His tongue slipped between her open lips, stopping the words.

Tara moaned as the sweetness and heat flooded into her mouth, overwhelming her, flowing down through her body to her breasts and belly and beyond, tightening her nerves with needs she didn't want to feel. Couldn't afford to feel.

Oh, please, no, she thought as she curled her fingers in the fabric of his shirt and leaned into him, offering her mouth fully. Completely. *No.*

"Yes," Gage murmured, as if she'd spoken aloud. "Oh, yes, that's what I want. Again." He repositioned his mouth on hers to make the joining deeper. "More."

Unable to resist his husky entreaty, his skillful, seductive mouth, Tara sighed in surrender and gave him what he wanted. She slid her hands up behind his head and opened her mouth wider beneath the onslaught of his, letting him have it all. Her lips and tongue; her sighs and low, soft moans; her warmth and sweetness and need. Everything.

Gage took it and savored it and gave it back tenfold, cherishing her mouth with his until both of them were breathless and panting. He lifted his lips from hers with a deep moan. "I want to make love to you," he growled, rubbing his hands up and down the soft sleek muscles of her back under her sweatshirt to touch as much of her as he could. "I want to feel you under me and all around me. Let me make love to you, Tara."

She went utterly still in his arms. *Love,* she thought, wondering why she was surprised he'd stoop to using that tired old line. *What does love have to do with this? What does love ever have to do with it?* "Why?"

"Why?"

"Yes, why? Why do you want to make love to me? You don't love me." The words were muffled against his cheek, blunting some of their bitterness. "I don't think you even like me very much. So why?"

"This is why." He kissed her again and, helplessly, she kissed him back. "And this." He covered her bare breast with his palm and the nipple rose to greet him. "And this," he murmured, sliding his other hand down to her bottom to press her against his straining erection. "Isn't that reason enough for *why* between two consenting adults?"

"Usually." The cynical tone of her voice wasn't an act this time; she wasn't even aware of it. "But it isn't love by any stretch of the imagination." She shot him a slanted look from under her lashes that had nothing of a flirt in it. "Even for an overheated male imagination."

He smiled indulgently and cuddled her closer, too caught up in his own feelings to realize that she wasn't just playing the game. "Didn't anyone ever tell you that you don't have to be *in* love to *make* love?"

"Dozens of people," she said flatly. "And they were all men." She drew her head back, out of range of his nuzzling lips. "I listened to one of them, once," she said, looking him square in the eyes. "It was one of the worst mistakes of my life."

His brows drew together. "What are you saying, Tara? That you expect vows of . . . what? Undying love and commitment before you'll go to bed with a man? Promises of wedding bells and happily ever after?"

Her short bark of laughter was bitter and un-amused. "God forbid!" she said fervently, denying—even to herself—that that's exactly what she wanted. What she had always wanted. "But I'd like there to be at least affection and respect. Friendship, maybe," she told him. "And a chance for something more."

"Something more?" His frown deepened with the beginnings of renewed suspicion. "What kind of something more?"

"Just..." she shrugged "...something more." She slid her hands down to his biceps and pushed, trying to draw farther back, out of his embrace, but he wouldn't let her go.

"You can't deny you want me," he insisted, focusing in on what he knew to be true and resolving to worry about the "something more" later, when the demands of his body weren't wreaking havoc with what was left of his intellect. "You kissed me back."

"My body wants you, yes," she admitted, since there was no hiding what her response had been, "but I don't. I told you I didn't. Before you ever started this, I told you I wasn't interested in getting involved," she said, rushing to get it all out before she lost her nerve—or before he overwhelmed her senses again. "But you wouldn't listen."

"I'm listening now."

"And I'm saying no. Please. We hardly know each other, and what we do know, we don't seem to like much." She pulled out of his arms and, this time, he let her go. "If that makes you mad, I'm sorry. But that's the way it has to be."

"Mad?"

"That after all—" she fluttered her hands back and forth between them "—*this*, I'm still saying no."

He shoved a hand through his hair. "It frustrates the hell out of me, I'll admit that, but make me mad?" He shook his head. "Angry isn't exactly how I'd describe my feelings at this particular moment."

"Then you're not going to make things difficult for me?"

"Difficult?" He cocked a questioning eyebrow at her. "Difficult how?"

"On the set."

He still looked blank.

"This is a Kingston production," she said simply, determined to get it all out now. She couldn't spend the next four weeks with it hanging over her head, wondering if each day on the set was going to be her last. "You're a Kingston. And I just said no."

Gage suddenly looked very formidable. "What you're suggesting has a very nasty name," he said, insulted that she would even think such a thing of him—even though he'd thought something very like it of her.

"Yes," she agreed. "But that doesn't stop it from happening."

"To you?"

Tara gave him a wry you-can't-possibly-be-that-naive look.

"Who?" he demanded.

"It isn't important."

"Who?"

"Really, Gage, it doesn't mat—oh, for heaven's sake," she cried, quailing a bit at the ferocious look in his eyes. She took a half step back. "It's something that happens all the time, on practically every set I've ever worked on. You learn to cope with it."

"Not on this set you don't," he said, his voice hard and unequivocal. "There's no casting couch at Kingston Productions. There never has been and there never will be. So you can relax on that score—your job doesn't depend on who you do or don't sleep with around here."

Tara let out a breath she didn't know she'd been holding.

"Just don't relax too much."

She looked up at that, renewed wariness in her wide eyes.

"I'm not going to threaten you with your job, no matter how frustrated I get or how often you say no. But that doesn't mean I've given up trying to get you flat on your back." He grinned suddenly, wolfishly, making her knees go weak all over again. "Or up against a wall. Or straddling me with those long legs of yours."

"Gage . . ."

"Don't looked so panicked, honey. I don't mean right now. We're going to be working together for at least a month on this picture. Maybe longer. I figure that'll give us more than enough time to develop some of that respect and affection you think is so necessary for sex. I respect you already, you know," he told her. "You're a hell of an actress. As for affection..." He reached out and lifted her chin. "I suspect you'd be real easy to develop affectionate feelings for," he said, brushing the pad of his thumb slowly over her moist lower lip. "In fact, I'm feeling real—" his voice dropped to a husky, suggestive whisper "—affectionate right now."

Tara shuddered in helpless response but managed to fight the urge to close her eyes and lean into him.

"You sure it's no?" Gage murmured.

"No." Her eyes flared wide at the sudden leap of heat and eagerness in his. "I mean, yes, I'm sure it's no."

He brushed his thumb over her lip again. "You don't sound sure."

"I am." She grabbed his wrist, telling herself to push his hand away and prove it. *I am. I am. I am!*

"You just keep telling yourself that, honey," Gage said softly, "and maybe you'll start to believe it. But I doubt it." He lifted her chin higher with the finger still curled under it, tilting her head even farther back so that she would have had to close her eyes to avoid looking at him. "You want me, Tara Channing," he said, staring into her eyes. "Almost as much as I want you. And we're both going to get what we want. Not as soon as

I'd like, maybe, but sooner than you think." He bent his head and kissed her—a hard, quick, possessive kiss that rocked her to her toes. "Think about it tonight while you're trying to sleep." And then he released her chin and turned on his heel, letting himself out of her trailer before she could utter a word in protest or response.

"SO," PIERCE SAID, looking up from the pile of papers he was studying when his older brother banged into the trailer they shared. "She turned you down."

Gage shot him a warning look and crossed over to the refrigerator to get himself the beer he'd told Tara he didn't want.

"Was it a definite not-on-your-life, over-my-dead-body, absolutely never no?" Pierce asked, obviously enjoying himself. "Or one of those maybe-if-you-beg-long-enough-I-might-reconsider nos?"

Gage popped the top of his beer and took a deep swallow. "What makes you think she said no?"

Pierce made a show of looking at the gold-and-stainless-steel watch on his wrist. "Twenty minutes," he said, as if that explained it. Which it did. "Even you couldn't manage a seduction in twenty minutes."

Except, Gage thought, staring down at the beer in his hand, that he very nearly had managed it. If he'd pushed just a little harder, been just a little more ruthless and a little less considerate of the ambivalence of her feelings, he'd be burning up in her arms right this minute instead of burning up with frustration.

"I knew she wouldn't make it easy for you."

Gage looked up to find his brother grinning at him with a look of satisfaction on his face. "Just how the hell do you know so much about what she will or won't do?" he growled.

"We're friends."

"Yeah." Gage took another swallow of beer. "So she said."

"What? You don't believe her?"

"Oh, I believe her, all right." But until Pierce had confirmed it, Gage realized he hadn't been entirely convinced.

"But?" Pierce prompted.

Gage shrugged, his big shoulders moving uneasily under his faded denim shirt. "I believe her," he said slowly, raising the beer to his lips for another swallow before continuing, "but I don't trust her."

Pierce sighed. Loudly. "She isn't the least bit like Alyssa."

Gage shot his brother another one of those warning looks. "I didn't say she was."

"Hell, Gage. You didn't have to say it. I know how your mind works. You didn't trust actresses much before you married that amoral female barracuda. Now you practically want 'em to sign a blood oath stating they don't want anything from you but your body and some cheap thrills before you'll get involved. And I use the term 'involved' only in its most basic sense."

"So—" Gage shrugged again "—I'm cautious where women are concerned."

"Cautious, hell," Pierce snorted. "You're as suspicious as a vice cop in a room full of paid informants."

He shook his head, giving his brother an admonishing look. "You'll never charm a lady like Tara with an attitude like that."

5

SO, OKAY, Gage thought, his gaze glued to Tara's expressive face as the eighth take of the next day's first scene unfolded on his monitor, *so maybe Pierce is right and you are a suspicious SOB. So what?*

As far as Gage was concerned, a little healthy suspicion was far better than allowing himself to be led around by the crotch again the way he had with Alyssa. If he was wrong about Tara, well, no harm done. But he didn't think he was wrong. Not completely, anyway.

Oh, she wasn't the conniving, fame-hungry deceiver his ex-wife was—she'd have to go a long way to top Alyssa in cunning and greed—but she was still an actress looking for stardom. And he was still Gage Kingston, a full partner in the most successful production company in Hollywood and eldest son of legendary director, Barry Kingston. More than one woman—both before and after the debacle of his marriage to Alyssa—had hoped to trade on her relationship with Gage for special considerations with his family's production company.

Before Alyssa, he'd always managed to look at it as just an unavoidable consequence of being a scion of movie royalty. Annoying, at times, but essentially harmless. But after Alyssa . . . ah, after Alyssa his attitude had changed dramatically.

He'd been young and stupid and she'd blinded him with her beauty and her special brand of seductive innocence that, in reality, wasn't innocent at all. Stubbornly oblivious to the fact that she was using him, he'd gone to bat for her with all the intensity of his fiercely loyal nature. He'd compromised himself for her, pulling strings he wouldn't have pulled for anyone else, getting her parts she couldn't have gotten on her own merits. He'd even come close to breaking with his family over her. And, then, when he'd finally been forced to realize her talent didn't even begin to equal her sex appeal, when he'd finally stopped trying to pressure his family into giving her roles she couldn't handle and wasn't right for, she'd betrayed him. Both as an actress and as a woman.

Even then, it had still taken him a while to accept that his beautiful, seductive, charming wife wasn't the misunderstood innocent he'd thought her, but a heartless schemer with the morals of an alley cat. He'd fought hard against the knowledge, hating to admit, even to himself—*especially* to himself—that she'd been using him from the very start, that he'd *let* her use him, which was far worse to his way of thinking. The final break had come when she went public with her discontent and her betrayals, spitefully dragging him and his entire family through the slime with her.

The tabloids had had a field day with the juiciest Kingston scandal to come down the pike in more than fifteen years.

And Gage had vowed never to let himself be taken in by another woman who might possibly want anything from him other than a rousing good time in bed. Since there were a lot of women—even in Hollywood—who were happy to take him on that basis, he hadn't had any trouble keeping that vow.

Until three days ago.

Until that precise instant when he'd looked into his monitor and seen Tara Channing's exquisite face staring back at him with its intriguing blend of guileless vulnerability and scorching sexuality. It had hit him right between the eyes.

Or right between the legs, he amended, knowing that was closer to the truth. *Wanting* it to be closer to the truth, because his attraction to her would be a lot easier to handle if it was just a case of hormones gone wild.

Why the first day's shooting should have been any different from the half-a-dozen other times he'd seen her on film, though, he didn't know. Maybe it was because he hadn't actually seen her in the flesh before that. Or maybe it was because . . .

Oh, hell, if he was being honest with himself—and he always tried to be honest with himself—he'd admit that he'd felt her sensual pull before. That's why his had been the one dissenting vote when the family was deciding on whether to offer the part of Yelena to Tara Channing; and why he'd reluctantly agreed to using her only after it had become apparent that the actress they'd initially signed would be better off in a drug rehab clinic. He had to admit he'd known something like this would happen if he got within sniffing distance of the luscious Ms. Channing

The problem was, what was he going to do about it?

If he was smart he'd accept her rejection and forget the whole damn thing. But he already knew he wasn't going to be smart about it.

He wanted her too much.

And, damn it, she wanted him!

And, despite the fact that she seemed determined to complicate what was essentially a very simple matter of basic biology with a lot of emotional baggage, he knew one thing: they were both going to get what they wanted. He just hoped to hell he wasn't going to be reduced to begging for it. Because, by God, he wouldn't!

"At least I hope I won't," he muttered, and swung his camera around to keep Tara framed in his monitor as she made her way through a make-believe farmers' market.

"Cut. Damn it, cut!" Hans hollered, jumping off his perch on the dolly just in time to avoid being hit in the head by the heavy camera housing. He nearly knocked the dolly grip over as he struggled to keep his footing on the frozen, snow-covered ground. "What in the *hell's* the matter with you people today?" he demanded, straightening to scowl at the set at large.

No one was foolhardy enough to answer.

"This is a simple scene, damn it." He threw the rolled-up script in his hand down in disgust. "Yelena walks through the farmers' market with her basket on her arm. She stops to see if there's any fresh fruit available at any price. There isn't. She buys some cabbage and potatoes. She looks longingly at the sugar, counts her money and doesn't buy any. Simple. You should be able to do it with your eyes closed. Hell, you should be able to do it in your sleep. From the way things have been going this morning, I think some of you *are* doing it in your sleep."

The regular members of the cast and crew looked down at the snowy ground or up at the gloomy, cloud-laden sky or at the remarkably realistic construction of the market stalls—anywhere but at the director. They were all hoping someone else would be singled out to be made an example of. The extras, nonactors hired locally to provide bodies for the crowd scenes, simply stared, enthralled by yet another fascinating aspect of moviemaking.

"And you, damn it," Hans bellowed, rounding on his cinematographer.

Gage could almost hear the collective sigh of relief; the victim had been selected. One who, moreover, could be counted on to fight back if he was pushed too far, freeing those not chosen from any guilt feelings they might have suffered for abandoning a helpless lamb to the lion. Almost as one, the cast and crew shuffled forward in order not to miss anything.

"That's the third time today you've lost track of where the action is," Hans began. "The *third* time." He waved his hand at the camera. "You nearly took my head off with that damned thing."

"Sorry," Gage mumbled, hoping Hans would let it go at that, knowing—from nearly fifteen years of having worked with the Swedish director—that he wouldn't.

Things hadn't been going well this morning, starting with the fact that Catering had forgotten the cheese Danishes at breakfast. And cheese Danishes were

Hans's favorite. Then, during the first run-through of the scene the weather had turned, the brilliant winter sky suddenly threatening snow. By ten-thirty, it was snowing lightly. The extras, who'd been bused to the location from the nearest town, which was nearly sixty miles away, would have to be bused back and paid for another day if they were sent home before the scene was completed. So Hans had decided to continue shooting. Snow, he'd declared, would add an extra touch of authenticity to the scene. On top of all that, nearly everyone had flubbed a line or missed a cue or overstepped a mark or just plain been someplace they shouldn't be when the cameras were rolling.

"Well, damn it, 'sorry' doesn't get it done," Hans snapped, giving full vent to the temper everyone knew had been building ever since Jeremy Dean had tried to flex his ego. "This production is costing twenty grand an hour—"

"Twenty-five," the A.D. said in a blatant effort to kiss up.

"Twenty-five thousand an hour," Hans said with relish. "Which means every minute costs in the neighborhood of—"

The A.D. tapped frantically at his calculator. "Four-hundred, sixteen dollars and sixty-six cents."

"Four hundred, sixteen dollars and sixty-six cents," Hans thundered in a deep theatrical voice that reminded everyone he'd started his career as a Broadway actor. "A *minute*. That's more than a lot of people in this country make in two weeks."

"It's five months' salary in Russia," Pierce added helpfully, obviously doing what he could to stir things up. "Maybe six."

Gage glared at him.

So did Hans, who didn't like to be interrupted when he was working up to a fear-inspiring bout of directorial histrionics. "And every time you screw up," he said to Gage, "that's a minimum—a *minimum* of—"

"Twelve thousand, four hundred, ninety-nine dollars and eighty cents," the A.D. said. "That's supposing it only takes thirty minutes to get back on track," he added before anyone could ask him how he'd arrived at the figure. "It could easily be more."

"That's over thirty-seven thousand dollars you've cost us so far today," Hans said.

"Thirty-seven thousand, four hundred, ninety-nine dollars and forty cents, to be precise," the A.D. amended.

"Over thirty-seven thousand dollars," Hans said, waving the assistant director away now that his usefulness was over. "Wasted. And all because your mind's in your pants instead of on your job."

Gage could feel the heat crawling up the back of his neck, but he struggled to hold on to his temper. He knew he deserved every word. He also knew exactly what Hans was trying to do with this pseudo-temperamental display. An emotional blowup would relieve the tension for everyone, allowing them to get back on track but, damn, Hans was getting a little personal here.

"I said I was sorry," Gage growled, doing his best to play along without losing his temper for real. It would be touch and go, though, if Hans made any more references to his . . . preoccupation with Tara.

"And I said 'sorry' doesn't get it," Hans bellowed. "I can't get a movie made when my cinematographer is off woolgathering with his libido."

"So what would get it?" Gage bellowed back, the look in his amber eyes warning one and all that he was close to losing it. "A written admission of culpability? A blood oath not to go—what was it you called it?— woolgathering again?"

"A little less attention paid to Miss Channing's admittedly remarkable physical attributes and a little more attention to the matter at hand would be enough, thank you," Hans said coolly. "Do you think you can manage that? Or should I ask someone else to handle your camera?"

Gage swore. Viciously.

The cast and crew retreated a cautious half step.

Hans smiled, satisfied he'd made his point and put the fear of God into all of them. "Let's try to do it right this time," he said, holding his hand out for the script the A.D. had picked up off the ground.

"Places!" the A.D. hollered. "Let's do it again."

THE NEXT DAY'S SHOOTING didn't go much better. They didn't have to work with any inexperienced extras, there was no complicated action and even the weather, though bitterly cold, was cooperating. All of which should have made things run a great deal smoother. Somehow, it didn't.

"You must go, my darling. You must," Tara said for the sixteenth time that day. She managed to make her voice tremble with love and fear, exactly the same way it had trembled the first time she'd said the words.

She was standing in a deserted alley between a make-believe bakery and a make-believe butcher shop in a dreary make-believe industrial town in a province of the new Russia. She had a knitted shawl wrapped around her head with the ends draping over the shoulders of a heavy calf-length coat. Her mittened hands clutched at her lover's arms. The bruise on her cheek and the small cut at the corner of her mouth were fake, of course, courtesy of Makeup. But the cold seeping up her legs from the frozen ground and the white puffs of breath misting the air each time she opened her mouth were real.

"It is too dangerous for you to stay." She glanced around furtively, fearfully, as if afraid she might have been followed. "Much too dangerous," she continued in an anguished whisper. "Yuri is . . ." Her voice trailed off and her lashes lowered to hide her eyes, silently but clearly conveying her disinclination to betray her brother even after his harsh treatment of her.

"Yuri is?" Pierce prompted, lifting her chin on his finger.

"Please," she said, refusing to look up. "I cannot. Even for you, I cannot."

"Yuri is?" he repeated.

She lifted her lashes slowly, reluctantly, revealing tears that gathered but did not fall. They made her eyes look like water-drenched jewels. "Yuri is young and passionate. And he does not believe in the new Russia."

"He's a communist, then?"

"There are many in Russia, still—" she said, defending her brother "—many who think the old ways are better and that the new regime will lead only to more trouble and bad times. There was always food in the shops, at least, under the old regime. Now it is...chaos and uncertainty. And there are many who would go back. If they could."

"What is he planning, Yelena?" Pierce demanded. His voice was soft and compassionate but as unyielding as steel; he would have his answers, even if it meant the woman he loved must betray her brother. "He and his radical communist friends, what are they planning?"

"I don't know."

His hands tightened on her shoulders. "Why do you protect him? Why?" He reached up and, very tenderly, touched her bruised cheek. His face twisted with anger. "After he did this to you?"

She turned her head away, ashamed for him to see the results of her brother's fury.

He held her still. "No, don't turn away from me, Yelena. Don't." He bent his head and touched his lips to the bruise on her cheek. "When this is over, I'm going to take you far away from here," he promised. "And no one will ever hurt you like this again. But you have to help me, my love. You have to tell me what he's planning so I can stop him and his friends before it's too late."

"I don't know what he is planning. Truly, I don't!" But she said it in such a way that anyone sitting in a darkened theater would know it was only a half-truth, an evasion meant to protect both her brother and her lover. "He does not tell me his plans. He does not trust me. I think he has me watched. He . . ." She let her eyes shift fearfully, her gaze drifting beyond her lover's face as if to check for spies in the darkening shadows of twilight.

Camera One was positioned just a few feet behind Pierce's shoulder for this close-up, emotional scene. Gage's camera. And he was behind it, staring at her through the filtered lens, projecting heat and wanting, and making her want in return, making her remember the sweet taste of his mouth on hers and the feel of his hands on her body. Her mind went blank but she tried anyway.

"He . . . ah, he . . ."

"Cut!"

"WE'RE GOING TO HAVE to let Bob roll film for Tara's close-up in this scene, Gage," Hans said to his cinematographer as they stood together in whispered conference behind the camera.

They'd done sixteen takes. Sixteen takes of what was a relatively simple, straightforward scene. It was an emotional scene, no doubt about it. A pivotal point in the plot. But it shouldn't have been this much trouble to shoot. There was no complicated action, no fancy camera angles, just a medium two-shot of a man and a woman, standing very still and staring into each other's eyes. Easy—except when you added the human element.

"She isn't going to get it, otherwise," Hans said wearily. "Not with you standing three feet away, staring at her as if she were a tall glass of iced tea and you were a man dying of thirst."

"I don't—" Gage began and then broke off as Hans narrowed his eyes at him. "Oh, hell, all right. Bob—" he called the second cameraman over "—take over here, will you? I'll handle the camera for the master shot."

Bob nodded and stepped behind Camera One.

Hans drew Gage a little away with him, out of earshot of anyone else. "I want you two to get this thing settled before much longer."

"Settled?"

"Settled," Hans stated firmly. "I don't care how you do it. Just do it. It's interfering with my movie."

"And what makes you think 'settling' it won't interfere more?"

"I'll leave it up to you to see that it doesn't."

"Oh, thanks very much," Gage said sarcastically, not sure whether he was annoyed or amused by his friend's interference in his private life. He decided he was both. "I appreciate your tact."

"And I'd appreciate your cooperation. Otherwise this picture is going to be over budget before we're a week into shooting." He rubbed a hand over the back of his neck. "And then I'll have Elise coming down on me like a ton of bricks."

Gage grinned at Hans's hangdog expression. His mother, the legendary French movie-star-turned-producer, had been the driving force behind Kingston Productions from the beginning. She had a well-deserved reputation for paying close attention to budgetary matters, especially during these recessionary times when even the major studios were forced to keep close tabs on financial matters or suffer the consequences. It was rare that any Kingston Productions project went more than a few thousand dollars over budget without Elise Gage demanding to know the reason why.

"I doubt she'd come out here herself to stomp on you," Gage said consolingly. He knew what it was to be on the wrong side of his mother's well-bred wrath. "Too cold." He grinned again. "She'd probably send Claire instead."

Hans snorted. "As if that sharp little sister of yours would be any easier to deal with." He rubbed at the ache in the back of his neck again. "It isn't just the money, anyway. With the political situation the way it is over there," he said, meaning in Russia and its former provinces, "this movie could be outdated before we get it to the screen."

"I doubt it," Gage consoled the director. "Those poor bastards are going to be sorting out the political situation over there for the next ten years, at least. I think your movie's safe."

"Tell that to your mother." Hans turned back to the set. "All right, people," he said, raising his voice to get everyone's attention. "Let's try to get it right this time. Before the light goes completely. Tara, my dear, you were perfect up until that last line. Just perfect. Do it exactly that way for me one more time and we can get this one in the can. All right?"

"Yes," Tara agreed, nodding. Her gaze slid to where Gage stood talking to the second cameraman. He looked up, meeting her eyes for one heated moment. She quickly looked away, forcing her attention back to the director. "I'm sorry about—"

"No need to be sorry. These things happen to everyone."

"Not to me." Tara shook her head. "I'm known as One Take Tara on the set of 'As Time Goes By,'" she said, referring to the afternoon soap opera on which she'd been appearing for the past two years.

"Just do your best, my dear, that's all I ask." Hans patted her shoulder lightly before turning to his male lead. "Let's see just a little more anguish and restrained fury when you touch her bruised cheek," he told Pierce. "You want to kill the bastard for hitting her but you're mad at yourself, too, for allowing it to happen. And because you know you're not going to be around to stop it from happening again until you've done your job. I want to see the war between love and duty in those laserlike baby blues."

I WILL DO IT PERFECTLY this time, Tara told herself as Hans checked camera angles and lighting one more time. *I will.*

They'd been shooting with day-for-night filters to simulate twilight, but they'd been removed once the sun had started to go. If they didn't get the scene in this take, Tara thought dismally, they'd end up having to add artificial light to get the desired effect. If they didn't all freeze to death first. A snow-covered Montana prairie was bone-chillingly cold in the daytime; after dark they'd be lucky not to get frostbite or hypothermia.

"Quiet on the set," the A.D. called out.

"Roll film for take seventeen," Hans ordered.

"Seventeen takes," Tara whispered to Pierce. Her tone was one of self-disgust. "I've never had to do sev-

enteen takes of anything. Not even in the very first time
I was in front of a camera."

Pierce squeezed her hands.

The clapper slammed down.

"And . . ." Hans pointed his rolled-up script at Tara.
"Action."

"You must go, my darling. You must."

As she said the words, Tara tried to think only of the
scene she was doing, to think only of Yelena Zdravkovich and her heart-wrenching dilemma. She tried to
take a page from Jeremy's total-immersion method of
acting and *become* Yelena, submerging herself into the
role as she never had before. It didn't work.

A part of her was still Tara Channing and she had a
dilemma of her own. Not as desperate as Yelena's, perhaps, but infinitely more real to her. And one she was
going to have to do something about. Soon.

"You have to tell me what he's planning so I can stop
him before it's too late," Pierce said, making her realize they'd nearly come to the end of the scene.

Somehow, despite her inner turmoil and complete
lack of concentration, she'd managed to deliver her
lines and respond appropriately to Pierce's. Thank
God!

"I don't know what he is planning. Truly, I don't!"
She gave a helpless little gasp, not quite a sob. It wasn't
in the script but it worked. "He does not tell me his
plans. He does not trust me." A picture of Gage flashed
through her mind, giving the line another layer of truth.
"I think he has me watched. He . . ." She remembered
to let her gaze scan the darkened alley before bringing
it back to Pierce's face. She closed her eyes tight for a

moment, as if fighting indecision and tears. When she opened them, they were clear and dry. Her decision was made. Both Yelena's and her own. "He is going to a meeting tonight. I am not sure where. At Feodor Bartlinksy's, I think. He is an important man in the village."

"The foreman at the machine factory."

"Yes." Her eyes asked him how he, a stranger to their small town, knew that but she didn't give voice to the question. "The foreman at the factory. He was important in the Party. People feared him because of it and he...I think that he liked to be feared. To be important. I think he would like to be that important again and that he drags Yuri and other young men into his dreams of glory."

Pierce lifted her hands, turning one so he could press his lips to the bare patch of skin below her mitten. "Thank you, my love." He turned the other wrist and kissed it, too. "Thank you for trusting me."

"You will save him, won't you?"

"Save him?"

"Yuri. He is not a bad boy. Not really. He is just young and confused and..." she touched her bruised cheek "...and his temper overrules him at times. Please," she pleaded, clutching at her lover's lapel. "Promise me you will save him from his foolishness."

Pierce looked at her for a long moment. "Yes," he promised. It was apparent from the expression in his eyes that he meant what he said, that he wasn't just mouthing empty words to please her. It was also clear that he would rather not have made the promise. "Yes, I'll save him. If I can."

"Cut," Hans said, his voice rich with satisfaction. "And print."

TARA WASTED NO TIME in implementing the decision she'd made. She left Pierce standing in the snow and walked over to where Gage stood talking to Hans and the second cameraman. "I'd like to speak to you," she said to him, ignoring the other two men as if they weren't there.

Gage lifted an eyebrow at her cool, imperious tone. It was so totally incongruous with her appearance—the voice of a titled aristocrat coming out of the mouth of a downtrodden working class Russian girl.

"Now, if it isn't too much trouble." If she waited, she thought, she might change her mind. "It will only take a minute."

"Excuse me, gentleman," Gage said, moving to follow her as she turned away. She held herself ramrod straight and her shoulders under the enveloping shawl and heavy coat were rigid and tense, as if she were bracing herself for something unpleasant. He wondered if she intended to lambaste him for the fact that the scene had required seventeen takes to perfect. Or, perhaps, she wanted to warn him not to let it happen again.

He put his hand on her elbow, stopping her forward progress. "You were as much to blame for what happened today as I was."

"Yes." She halted but didn't turn around. "I'm quite aware of that."

He couldn't hide his surprise and didn't try to. "You are?"

"Yes." She took a deep breath, steeling herself, and turned around to face him. "You were right."

Something in her voice told him she wasn't talking about who was to blame for the length of time it had taken to film the scene. "About what?"

"About me."

"Really?" He reached out to tuck a strand of sunset gold hair under the edge of the shawl that still wrapped her head. Though he hadn't consciously intended it as such, the gesture was one of tenderness, meant to calm whatever it was that was making her look so tense. "What about you?"

"I want you."

His hand stilled, his fingers tightening on her hair as every muscle in his body clenched in response to her words. *I want you*, she'd said. Glorious words. Words to make a man's blood heat and his head spin, except—why had they sounded so matter-of-fact? So cold? He dropped his hand. "And?" he said carefully. There had to be an *and* to that statement.

"And I've decided you're right," she said, staring at his throat. It was safer, less embarrassing, than looking into his amber eyes. "We're going to, ah . . . to have sex sooner or later. For some reason it seems inevitable. That being the case, I think we should do it now."

"Now?"

"If we wait until later, this movie is going to be seriously over budget and Hans is likely to commit homicide or suicide, or both. I'd rather just get it over with and out of the way now before it interferes any more."

"Over with? Out of the way?" His hands flexed at his sides and he put them behind him, slipping them, palms outward, into the back pockets of his jeans. It was that, he thought, or wrap them around her neck. "That's an awfully cold way of looking at it."

"Isn't that the way you look at it? Coldly, I mean? Just plain sex, right? No strings. No commitments. No promises." Her eyes flickered up to his and held for just a moment. They were full of vague accusations and stubborn determination and a confused sort of anger, as if she weren't quite sure *who* to be mad at for the situation she found herself in. "You want me," she said, looking away again. "And, as you said, I want you. So we go to bed together and both of us get what we want. What could be colder than that?"

"Honey, the last thing I feel when I think of crawling into bed with you is cold."

Tara debated that a moment, feeling anything but cold herself. "Is that a yes or no?"

"I haven't heard a question yet."

That brought her eyes back to his. The anger flashed brighter this time. Hotter. More focused. "You're determined to make this hard on me, aren't you?"

"Seems fair. You're making it hard on me."

Unable to stop herself, she glanced down. She was, it seemed, very definitely making it hard on him. Her face flamed. "Oh—" Words seemed to stick in her throat and, suddenly, it was all just too much. She couldn't do it. She didn't know what had made her think she could, what had made her think she wanted to. "Never mind. Just forget I said anything. Just for—"

He reached out and grabbed her arm as she whirled away. "Yes," he said fiercely. "The answer is yes."

She stilled instantly but he could feel her trembling beneath his fingers, quivering like a small animal in a trap. He told himself to open his hand and let her go. But he couldn't.

"When?" he demanded.

She hesitated for a long moment. *Tell him never. Save yourself and tell him never.* "Tonight," she heard herself say. "In my trailer. Give me time to shower and have something to eat, and then . . ."

"Seven o'clock?"

"Yes," she agreed. "Seven would be fine." Eight would be better. Or nine. Or never. "Just let yourself in. I'll leave the door unlocked. I'd appreciate it if you'd be—" she glanced up at him uncertainly "—discreet."

He frowned at that. What in the hell did she think he'd do? Stand outside her door and give a Tarzan yell while he pounded on his chest and demanded that she let him in? It made him mad that she'd even question his discretion. Damn mad. But not, he admitted wryly, mad enough to throw her offer back in her face.

"Seven o'clock, then," he said, letting go of her arm.

She nodded once and turned toward her trailer.

Gage stood where he was, watching her as she picked her way over the snowy ground. He was aroused and furious and, yes, a little...hurt. Although that, he was sure, was just from the injury to his pride. He'd never been issued quite such a *grudging* invitation to a woman's bed. She'd made it more than clear that though she'd made the offer, she would really prefer that he didn't take her up on it.

Hell, if he was smart, he thought, he wouldn't take her up on it. At least, not tonight. If he was smart, he'd make her wait and worry and . . . Oh, hell, who was he kidding? Any brains he may at one time have possessed had turned to mush the first time he'd looked into Tara Channing's slanted cat's eyes and seen the raging heat of his own desire reflected back at him.

6

TARA HAD UNDRESSED and creamed off her fake bruise and the cut at the corner of her mouth, and she was standing under the spray of a too-hot shower when the panic hit her. It came hard and fast, stealing her breath away and making her feel as if she'd had the wind knocked out of her. She hugged her arms around her midsection and curled over, sagging back against the cool white tiles of the shower stall as she fought to control her breathing.

She hadn't been this scared, she realized in amazement, since Bobby Clay Bishop told her she was going to have to face the consequences of her stupidity alone.

"Nonsense," she told herself firmly, forcing herself upright through sheer strength of will. She took two deep, calming breaths and reached out to adjust the water temperature to a more comfortable level. "Absolute, utter nonsense." There was nothing even remotely similar between then and now.

Then, she had been a terrified seventeen-year-old girl, ruing the fact that she'd let herself be pressured into proving her love for a boy she'd already begun to realize had never really loved her at all. Now, she was a grown woman of twenty-five who was getting ready to go to bed with a man she wanted much more than she'd ever wanted Bobby Clay—or anyone else, for that matter.

And that, she thought, her hand still on the chrome handle of the shower, was the crux of her panic.

The wanting.

She hadn't invited Gage to her bed for any of the cold and seemingly logical reasons she'd given him—or herself. Oh, the movie was important, certainly, but delayed shooting schedules and a director's tantrums weren't enough to drive her into any man's arms. Not by a long shot. It was the wanting that was doing that.

It clawed at her insides like a living thing, making a mockery of her efforts to be sophisticated and blasé about it. And she wanted, very badly, to be as sophisticated and blasé about it as Gage Kingston obviously was, to keep up the protective facade she'd built so carefully over the past few years.

It was just a little recreational sex, she reminded herself, recalling the arguments men had used more times than she could count. Just basic biology; a quirky chemical reaction between two people; a game men and women had been playing since the beginning of time; a purely physical encounter with no messy emotional complications.

Maybe it would be easier that way.

No promises but no lies, either. No commitment but no unmet expectations. And no strings to tie you up in knots after it was over. Because it was always over, sooner or later. It was a lesson she'd learned at her mother's knee, one that had been reinforced by her own bitter experience. Men left. Men always left. And women were left behind, nursing broken hearts and broken dreams and wondering what they'd done wrong.

So maybe the male of the species had the right idea, after all. If you expected nothing more than physical pleasure from a relationship then you couldn't be disappointed when that was all you got. Easy. Yes, it would definitely be easier that way, she decided, reaching for the shower gel.

She shampooed her hair and shaved her legs and, after she got out of the shower, rubbed flower-scented cream into her damp body, all the while telling herself that she wasn't doing any of it to entice or please Gage but to boost her own shaky self-confidence. Wrapped in a fluffy peach-colored towel with another around her head, she stood in front of the bathroom mirror and debated the use of cosmetics. Maybe she should dab on just a little blusher to give some color to her cheeks and, perhaps, a dash of mascara to define her eyes and, then—*no*, she thought vehemently, abruptly deciding that painting on a more glamorous face would be like admitting that she didn't think the one she'd been born with was good enough for him.

What to wear caused another problem. If she got dressed, she'd just have to undress again—with him watching her. Or he'd want to undress her himself and she didn't think she could stand that, either. The process of undoing buttons and hooks and zippers would draw the whole thing out, making the tension unbearable. Waiting naked in bed might be more to the point, but it would be blatant and crass—and totally beyond her capabilities at this point. A nightgown, she decided, but nothing slinky or lacy or see-through, nothing that screamed *sex*. Not that she had one like that, anyway.

She slept in white cotton nightgowns with delicate pin-tucked bodices embroidered with tiny wildflowers or embellished with cotton-lace insets and rows of tiny mother-of-pearl buttons. They had long sleeves that ended in a narrow self-ruffle at her wrist or wide eyelet bands threaded with pastel ribbons that went over her shoulders and left her arms bare. Most of them had deep flounces at the hem that covered her legs nearly to the ankles. All of them had matching robes that were just as sweetly feminine and old-fashioned as the gowns. And none of them, she realized, were what a man would expect a notorious "other woman" to wear to bed.

Well, it couldn't be helped, she thought, pulling one of them on over her head and topping it with a robe that tied at her neck with a pale blue ribbon. Decently covered, with her damp, towel-dried hair waving down around her shoulders, she contemplated the question of where to wait for him. In bed? Curled up in a corner of the white leather sofa in the living room, pretending to read, perhaps? Should she open some wine? Set out something to nibble on? Put on some music? Light some candles or—

She stood stock-still in the middle of the compact little kitchenette of her trailer with her fingers around the refrigerator handle, aghast at what she'd been about to do. This wasn't a romance. It was an affair. No, not even that. It was . . . oh, Lord, she didn't know what it was. A one-night stand, maybe. Probably. But it most definitely was *not* a romance. No matter how much she might want it to be.

"Fool," she said aloud, yanking her hand away from the refrigerator. "Stupid fool."

She switched off the kitchen light and the one next to the sofa in the small living room and went back into the bedroom to sit on the edge of the satin-covered bed. Blindly reaching for the hairbrush on the nightstand, she deliberately shut down her mind, trying not to think at all, and began the long, soothing process of brushing her hair dry.

GAGE SHOWERED AND SHAVED and slapped on a light woodsy cologne, ignoring his brother's smart-assed remarks about first dates and "performance" nerves and the best ways to impress women. Even after he'd made himself slow down and eat the pasta and vegetable dish Pierce had thrown together, he was still ready a full thirty minutes early. He left the trailer, anyway, deciding a long cold walk in the frigid night air just might cool him down enough to keep him from jumping on Tara the minute he saw her. He wanted her beneath him, and soon, but he wanted to accomplish the deed with a little finesse. More finesse, anyway, than she'd shown in issuing her invitation.

It was precisely seven o'clock when he opened her trailer door. The living room and kitchenette were dark and shadowed. He navigated them silently, eagerly, tossing his heavy sheepskin jacket onto the leather sofa as he headed for the warm pool of light shining through the open door at the rear of the trailer. His pulse leaped wildly at the thought that she was waiting for him in bed. She'd be soft and sleek and beautifully naked, as hot and eager as he was.

But she wasn't.

He stopped in the doorway, something warm and dangerously tender mixing with the passion in his blood at the sight of her.

The plush little bedroom was a standard Hollywood fantasy—delicate white-and-gilt furniture, a white satin bedspread heaped with plump velvet-and-satin pillows, pale peach walls and ankle-deep peach carpet, crystal lamps with pleated white shades on either side of the bed, a dreamy Impressionist flower painting in mauve and lavender and peach on the wall. It was a room Jean Harlow or Marlene Dietrich—or Madonna—would have felt completely at home in, a glamorous room meant for seduction and sin.

The woman on the bed was another fantasy entirely. She sat with one hand resting, palm up, in her lap. Her eyes were closed as if she were dreaming. Her head was tilted to one side as she slowly drew a silver-backed brush through her glorious mane of hair. She was wearing a plain white nightgown with long, full sleeves and a pale blue bow that tied at the base of her throat. In it, she radiated all the innocence and sweetness of an old-fashioned bride. The kind of bride, he thought, who would have worn white on her wedding day and white on her wedding night because she deserved to.

He wondered if she'd created the impression deliberately and, cynical to the core, decided she probably had. But the knowledge that she was trying to manipulate his responses didn't kill the tenderness building in him or stop him from crossing the room to her. Nothing could have stopped him.

"Tara."

She started at the sound of his voice, her eyes going wide as she looked up at him. "Oh—it's you." The brush stilled in her hand. "I didn't hear you come in."

"You told me to be discreet."

"Yes. Yes, I did. Thank you."

He smiled at her grave seriousness. "You're welcome."

"Well, I guess we should . . ." She made a move as if to stand up.

"No. Stay." He put a hand on her shoulder to keep her where she was and plucked the hairbrush out of her nerveless fingers. "Allow me."

"Oh, no, I—"

"I know this probably wasn't on your agenda for this evening," he said, putting one knee on the bed beside her. "It wasn't on mine, either." He angled his body so he was a little behind her. "But indulge me." He brought the brush down through her hair, slowly, following it with his other hand. The strands of sunset-tinged, honey-gold silk reacted as if they were alive, lifting to coil and cling to his fingers. "Beautiful," he breathed. "You have incredibly beautiful hair."

Tara sat very still, afraid to speak, afraid to move in case he stopped what he was doing. She was used to having other people's hands in her hair. Used to other people combing and teasing and fluffing her hair into some kind of order. But not since she was a child had anyone just brushed it. It felt wonderful. Soothing, almost tranquilizing, slowly coaxing the tension from her body. Fleetingly she wished Gage would be content to do nothing else but brush her hair all night long. Nothing else, just brush her hair, making her feel pampered and safe and strangely cherished.

"It's so soft," Gage murmured. "I've never known a woman's hair to be so soft." He dropped the hairbrush onto the bed and took great handfuls of the silky stuff into his fists. "Or so thick." He bent his head and buried his face in it, breathing deeply of the wildflower fragrance that scented it. "Or so sweet." His hands dropped to her shoulders and squeezed. "Tara."

She tensed. This was it. They would begin. She told herself there was nothing to be afraid of. She'd done this before; she knew exactly what to expect. But she trembled anyway.

"Don't be afraid," he said into her hair. "I won't hurt you."

"I know," she said, knowing—no matter what he said—that he would. Knowing, too, that they didn't mean the same kind of hurt." It's not that."

"Then what?"

"I'm . . ." What did men want to hear at a time like this? She tried to recall the lines—any lines—from the countless love scenes she'd played in her career. "I'm excited, is all. And . . . eager."

"Are you?" Gently he tugged her head back by the hair so he could look down into her face. His eyes searched hers. "Are you really?"

"Yes," she said. And it was true. Almost. She *was* excited. And eager. And afraid. So afraid. He was being gentler than she'd expected. More tender. Infinitely sweeter. She'd anticipated a rougher passion, a careless disregard for her sensitive woman's feelings, something on a more purely physical level. Not callousness, exactly, but not this aching tenderness, either. She had no defenses against tenderness. She didn't want it. She couldn't cope with it.

She reached up and pulled her hair from his grasp. "Let me show you," she murmured, suddenly frantic to put a stop to his debilitating gentleness. Raw passion was what they felt for each other. *All* they felt for each other. To imagine it as anything else was to invite heartbreak. She stood and turned toward the bed to face him, giving him a look of practiced seduction as she reached up and slowly pulled the blue bow at her throat loose. "Let me show you how eager I am."

"No." His voice was harsh in the dimly lit room. "Damn it, no." He took her hands in his and jerked them back down to her sides. "I don't want that."

"But I—"

"No," he said again. "I don't want a cheap simulation of passion. An act." His wife had given him all the false coin he could stomach; he didn't want more of the same from this woman. Ever. "And if that's all you have to give, then I've changed my mind." He lifted his knee off the bed and threw her hands away from him. "I'm not interested."

Unable to stop herself, Tara reached out and grasped his sleeve. "It isn't an act, Gage. I—" She didn't know what else to say. "It's not an act."

"I've seen that hollow little smile on the TV screen every time Jessica—" Jessica was the scheming secretary Tara played on the afternoon soap "—sets out to seduce some poor sap out of his millions." He shook her hand off. "So don't tell me it's not an act."

"It isn't. Not the way you mean." She clasped her hands in front of her and stared down at them, wondering why she didn't just take the out he offered and be done with it. But she couldn't. Her desire for him was apparently much stronger than her fear of what would happen if she gave in to that desire. "I just wanted to please you, is all. And I thought..." she sighed. "It's like something Rita Hayworth was supposed to have said, a long time ago in an interview when someone asked her why her relationships didn't seem to work out. She said men always thought they were going to bed with Gilda but they woke up with her and..."

"And?"

"I know what I look like, Gage," she said, still staring at her hands. "I know what men expect from a woman who looks like me. I know what *you're* expecting. And I was just trying to..." she lifted one shoulder in an uncertain little shrug "... to live up to your expectations."

He stared at her bent head for a long moment. "You thought I expected you to act like a soulless little sex doll?" he said softly, incredulously. "Like some overinflated centerfold come to life?"

She looked up at that, a quick, frankly skeptical look from underneath her lashes. "Didn't you?"

He laughed ruefully, not sure whether to be insulted or amused. "Hell, no!"

"Then what—" She licked her lips nervously and looked down at her hands again. "What do you want me to be, Gage?"

He was silent for another long moment, staring at her bent head, wondering if she could possibly be as shy and uncertain as she seemed; wondering if he dared believe she was real; wondering, too, why in the hell it mattered so damned much.

"Just be yourself," he said, finally, almost wearily, as if he didn't really believe it was possible.

Tara shook her head. "You don't really want that."

"Yes," he insisted. "I do. I don't want an act or a pretense of passion. I'm sick to death of pretense." He reached out and touched her cheek lightly, stroking the soft color that bloomed there with the backs of his fingers. "I just want you to be yourself. Just give me your honest, natural responses without pretending and without trying to anticipate whatever it is you think I might want." He trailed his fingers beneath her chin, urging her to look at him. "Can you do that?"

She stared up at him mutely, unsure what to say. Her natural responses were sadly lacking. If that's what he wanted from her—if that's all he would let her give him—he was going to be badly disappointed. And she was going to be badly hurt when he let her know just how disappointed he was.

"Tara? Can you forget you're an actress for a couple of hours and just be yourself?"

"I can try," she murmured, thinking that maybe his was the best way, after all. One night with the real Tara Channing and he wouldn't want another one. He'd stop wanting her, stop staring at her with desire and speculation in his hot amber eyes, stop making her want him.

She'd be safe from her own desires, then. Safe from all the frightening, unfamiliar yearnings that assailed her each time their eyes met.

"Don't try," he urged. "Just be." His fingers curved, caressing the delicate skin under her jaw, sliding around to capture the back of her neck. His eyes blazed, hot and greedy with barely controlled lust as he pulled her to him. "God, I want you," he whispered, and tilted her face up to his.

His kiss was much like the first one he'd given her—fierce and voracious in its intensity—and, yet, not like it, too. It wasn't mindless or demanding. It didn't make her feel as if she were being driven toward unconditional surrender with no will of her own. It felt, instead, as if he were pouring all his passion, all his burning need and desire into her, and then patiently, persistently, inexorably urging her to return it with all the passion she herself possessed.

Tara tried to respond in a natural, honest way. She parted her lips under the onslaught of his, offering the sweet recesses of her mouth to the skillful caress of his tongue. Somehow, it wasn't enough. There was something more he wanted from her . . . something else she knew she should be giving him. . . .

And then his tongue stroked hers, softly, erotically, sending a jolt of pure feeling through her. He withdrew before she could return the caress. Between one heartbeat and the next, Tara forgot to monitor her responses, forgot to wonder what he wanted, and simply reacted to the dawning of her own needs. Her head fell back, her mouth opened wider, her tongue darted forward to tangle with his. She leaned into him and lifted

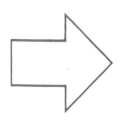

NO COST! NO OBLIGATION TO BUY! NO PURCHASE NECESSARY!

PLAY "LUCKY 7"
AND GET AS MANY AS FIVE FREE GIFTS . . .
HOW TO PLAY:

1. With a coin, carefully scratch off the silver box at the right. This makes you eligible to receive two or more free books, and possibly another gift, depending on what is revealed beneath the scratch-off area.

2. Send back this card and you'll receive brand-new Harlequin Temptation® novels. These books have a cover price of $2.99 each, but they are yours to keep absolutely free.

3. There's no catch. You're under no obligation to buy anything. We charge nothing—ZERO—for your first shipment. And you don't have to make any minimum number of purchases—not even one!

4. The fact is thousands of readers enjoy receiving books by mail from the Harlequin Reader Service®. They like the convenience of home delivery. . . they like getting the best new novels before they're available in stores . . . and they love our discount prices!

5. We hope that after receiving your free books you'll want to remain a subscriber. But the choice is yours—to continue or cancel, anytime at all! So why not take us up on our invitation, with no risk of any kind. You'll be glad you did!

This lovely Victorian pewter-finish miniature is perfect for displaying a treasured photograph—and it's yours absolutely free—when you accept our no-risk offer.

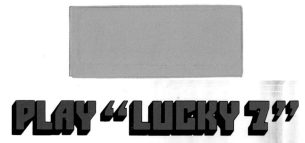

PLAY "LUCKY 7"

**Just scratch off the silver box with a coin.
Then check below to see which gifts you get.**

YES! I have scratched off the silver box. Please send me all the gifts for which I qualify. I understand I am under no obligation to purchase any books, as explained on the back and on the opposite page.

142 CIH AKWR
(U-H-T-07/93)

NAME

ADDRESS   APT

CITY   STATE   ZIP

7	7	7	WORTH FOUR FREE BOOKS PLUS A FREE VICTORIAN PICTURE FRAME
🍒	🍒	🍒	WORTH FOUR FREE BOOKS
⬤	⬤	⬤	WORTH THREE FREE BOOKS
🔔	🔔	🍒	WORTH TWO FREE BOOKS

Offer limited to one per household and not valid to current Harlequin Temptation® subscribers. All orders subject to approval.

© 1990 HARLEQUIN ENTERPRISES LIMITED

PRINTED IN U.S.A.

GET YOUR FREE GIFTS NOW! MAIL THIS CARD TODAY!

her hands to his waist. They hovered there for a moment, brushing up and down along his sides as if she couldn't quite decide what to do. Then she moaned and her arms went around him, her hands splayed wide against his broad back to hold him to her.

Gage murmured in satisfaction and pleasure, shifting his own arms to bring her higher and closer against him, and went on kissing her as if he never intended to stop. He kissed her with passionate extravagance and unselfish thoroughness, using his lips and tongue and teeth to nuzzle and lick and nibble as if her mouth were a rare, succulent fruit meant to be savored for as long as possible. He kissed her as if he would be utterly content to do it for the rest of his life.

It was Tara, finally, who took their embrace to the next step.

She reached down and behind her—with her mouth still pressed to his—and grasped his wrist, guiding his hand up under the fabric of her robe to cover her nightgown-draped breast. Gage groaned into her mouth and flexed his fingers against her soft, giving flesh.

Tara whimpered and pressed herself more deeply into his hand.

"Yes," he murmured, lifting his mouth from hers to touch his lips to her cheeks and temples and the delicate skin of her eyelids. He brushed his thumb across her nipple, bringing it to turgid, aching life beneath the fabric of her cotton gown. "Oh, yes."

Tara whimpered again, murmuring his name, and tilted her head back, unconsciously offering him more of herself. Gage bent his head even farther, dragging his lips down the exquisite line of her jaw and the arch of her throat, nudging aside the loosened blue bow and the wide lace-trimmed collar of her robe to nuzzle his face against the fragrant curve between her neck and shoulder.

They were panting softly, clutching each other tightly, aching for more. So much more.

"Touch me," they both pleaded at the same time, as if the identical need had burst upon them simultaneously.

Gage kneaded the soft breast under his hand. "I am."

"No," Tara whispered. "Under my clothes. Against my bare skin. I need—"

"Yes." Gage worked his free hand between them and jerked at the buttons on his denim work shirt, tearing some of them loose in his haste. "Against my skin." He took her right hand in his and brought it to his chest, pressing her palm flat against the hard curve of his pectoral muscle. "Here."

The contact was electric, holding them both stock-still for a moment to savor the feeling; his hard, hair-covered chest, warmed by his furiously beating heart and the pounding heat of his blood; her small, slender palm, soft and delicate and cool against his skin. Gage trailed the hand still resting on her breast to her shoulder, pushing back the edge of her robe and sliding down the wide neckline of her white lawn nightgown so he could cup the soft fullness of her bare breast. It was warm and lush, creamy white against his tanned skin, intensely feminine against his long, masculine fingers. The nipple was a deep red, as tempting and perfect as a sun-ripened cherry. He could feel her heart beating like a small wild bird against his palm.

He smiled at her. "This feels good."

"Yes," she said. "It does."

"It could feel better."

"Yes." Her smile almost matched his. "I think maybe it could."

"Only maybe?"

"I'm really not very good at this, Gage," she said seriously, sweetly, standing there with her hand on his chest and his cupping her breast. "At sex, I mean. But I want you. More than I've ever wanted any man."

He felt a wild thrill shoot through him at her softly spoken admission, but he forced himself to hold back from acting on it. "And?" he prompted, knowing from the look in her eyes that there was more.

"And I'm afraid I'll disappoint you."

He considered that for a moment. "Not live up to my expectations, you mean?" he asked, remembering what she'd said to him earlier.

"Yes."

He shook his head. "Impossible."

"How can you be so sure of that?"

He rolled his thumb over her nipple and watched her shiver in helpless response. "That's how."

"But—"

"That," he interrupted, lifting his other hand to touch her hair, "and the fact that I don't expect you to *do* anything or *be* anything. I haven't asked you to perform for me like some well-trained call girl." He tucked a strand of hair behind her ear, smoothing it back with gentle strokes that soothed and aroused at the same time. "Nothing but honest responses, remember?"

Tara nodded, slowly, her cheek brushing against the vulnerable inside of his wrist. "Honest responses," she agreed, and reached up with both hands to push his shirt off his broad shoulders.

They undressed each other without haste, taking the time to touch and stroke, wordlessly admiring what they uncovered. Pastel ribbons were untied and left dangling over the sweet flesh they bared. A leather belt was pulled through worn denim belt loops and dropped to the floor. Shoes were toed off and discarded. A zipper was lowered and left gaping open, exposing soft, springy hair to the hesitant but inquisitive touch of feminine fingertips. Tiny mother-of-pearl buttons were undone with trembling eagerness, then abandoned for the lush treasures that lay beneath. Soft fabric whispered over warm skin, followed by the gentle brush of a callused hand over tender curves.

And, then, when . . . finally . . . they were both naked and unbearably aroused, aching for completion, Gage lifted her in his arms and gently laid her down on the white satin bedspread.

"Honest responses," he said as he came down on top of her.

"Honest responses," she echoed, winding her arms around his neck to pull him to her.

He'd meant to enter her then, taking them both where they wanted to go without any further delay, but she was trembling and deliciously shy and he felt, suddenly, like a man with his virgin bride in his arms. He didn't question the feeling this time but went with it instead. He slipped a cradling arm under her shoulders and kissed her again, lingeringly, shifting his weight to one side so he could run his hand down the length of her body.

She stirred beneath him. "Gage?" she murmured uncertainly, knowing he had been intending something else when he came down on top of her, wondering what she had done to make him change his mind.

"Relax," he whispered, still stroking her. "Just relax and let it happen."

"But—"

"No, buts," he ordered, and kissed her into silence.

She was soft everywhere he touched her, soft and incredibly giving beneath the uncertainty and hesitation. Her mouth was avid and open under his, her tongue as eager as his to explore. Her arms were curled around his neck, her hands moving restlessly on his shoulders as if she didn't know what else to do with them. Her magnificent breasts were full and swollen with need, the nipples as hard as little pearls beneath the brush of his thumb. The fine soft skin of her stomach quivered when he caressed it. The muscles in her smooth thighs trembled when his fingers trailed between them. He brushed his palm across the curling golden red hair that covered her woman's mound and felt her stiffen.

"It's okay," he soothed, drawing one finger up and down the crevice where her hip and thigh joined. "Just let yourself relax." His voice was husky with need, smoky with desire. He ran his finger up and across and down again, outlining triangular the shape of the hair that grew there. "Just relax and open your legs for me,

Tara," he coaxed, trying to keep his voice soft and un-demanding but feeling as if he might explode in the next second if she didn't do as he asked. "Please."

She hesitated for another moment, trembling with indecision and deep, feminine uncertainty. What if she disappointed him?

"Tara, sweetheart, *please*," he whispered raggedly, sounding as if he were dying of want for her.

She sighed and parted her thighs, trusting herself to him and her own natural, honest responses, hoping it would be enough.

It was. More than enough.

He touched her tenderly, with a kind of reverence, parting her slick, silky folds with an instinctive, en-tirely masculine sort of gentleness that took full ac-count of her woman's fears and vulnerabilities. He circled the entrance to her body with thoroughness and care, brushing his fingers over her clitoris until it throbbed with exquisite, unbearable sensitivity.

Tara lay very still, absorbing the feelings he evoked in her, trembling all over as they rippled through her body with the heat and speed of a firestorm across a bone-dry summer prairie. She'd never felt this way be-fore. Never truly believed it was possible to feel this way. Her hands tightened, her fingers digging into the smooth, hard muscles of his shoulders as he inserted the tip of one finger into her body.

"Good?"

"Yes." Her head rolled against the satin spread. "Oh, yes."

"It's going to get even better," he promised.

She didn't know how it could, didn't know how she would stand it if it did. And then he bowed his back, bringing his head down to her breast, and took her nipple into his mouth, pushing two fingers deep into her body at the same time.

Tara's hips lifted off the bed, undulating in response, and he felt all her delicate, feminine muscles begin to quiver and spasm around his fingers. "You're fantastic," he breathed, overwhelmed and gratified by her intemperate reaction to his touch.

Tara felt her heart open wide and she stiffened and cried out against it, clamping her thighs together over his hand, as if controlling the floodgates of her physical response would control her emotional one as well. But it was too late. She was flying, soaring above herself, freed of her inhibitions and fears and the strict guard she put on her heart by his tenderness and care.

"No," she moaned, belatedly realizing what she'd allowed to happen. "Oh, no."

"Oh, yes," Gage said, urging her higher with his hands and his voice and his warm mouth at her breast. "Let it go. Let it out."

"Oh, no. *Please*," she cried, clutching at him, trying to hold it back.

She might have made it, might have been able to hold herself inviolate, if he hadn't chosen that moment to lift himself over her and join his body to hers in one powerful thrust of possession. She couldn't hold anything back then, couldn't temper her response to protect herself against the pain that was sure to follow this ecstasy. *This* was what she had instinctively been afraid of, she realized, as she lifted her hips to meet his thrusts.

She'd known—somehow she'd known!—that he could make her feel like this.

Every honest, natural response she had came tumbling out in one long, inarticulate cry as she fell over the precipice into bliss. Emotion overwhelmed her completely—all her suppressed passions and needs, all the excitement she'd tried to deny existed between them, and a wondrous, inexplicable, ridiculous feeling of incandescent joy—until there was nothing in her mind and her heart but him. Helplessly she arched her lush body under the driving, powerful, yet exquisitely tender thrusts of his hips and let it take her where it would.

THEY CAME DOWN from the heights slowly, both of them panting for long moments, struggling to catch their breaths and steady their erratic heartbeats. Gage recovered first, lifting himself to his elbows to look down at the woman beneath him. He smiled, masculine pride filling him at the sight of her.

Her cheeks were flushed and damp. Her hair was a wild cloud spread out on the tufted white satin beneath her head. Her exotic aquamarine eyes were wide and luminous with spent passion. Her perfect lips were moist and parted, as if ready for his kiss.

He felt himself getting hard all over again. Wanting her all over again.

He lifted his hand and brushed at the strands of hair that clung to her damp cheeks. "And you said you weren't any good at this," he teased, and bent his head to kiss her.

7

"WE DIDN'T USE ANYTHING," Gage muttered into her neck, coming back to reality rather more quickly this time than he had the first.

"Hmm?" Tara murmured lazily, still a bit dazed from the overload of emotion engendered by her second explosive climax of the evening. She stroked his back indolently, lost in the rosy glow of passion's aftermath. "We didn't what?"

Gage lifted his head from the warmth of her neck to look down at her. "We didn't use anything. Birth control," he added when she just stared at him. "Unless you . . . ?"

"No." Her caressing hands stilled on his back as the sense of his words got through to her. "Oh, no. I didn't." She couldn't have, even if she'd remembered the need for it, for the simple reason that she didn't have anything to use. "I'm sorry, Gage, I—"

"It's not your fault. It's mine. Damn," he exploded, "I've got half a dozen Trojans in the pocket of my jeans and I completely forgot about them." He looked as if he couldn't believe his own stupidity and carelessness. "Just completely lost my head."

"I'm sorry," Tara said, her voice small and miserable, the sublime contentment of a few moments before shattered. No matter what he said now, she knew whose fault it was going to be if something happened. Hers. Contrary to whatever notions of equality men and society paid lip service to, in the end, it was always the woman's responsibility when birth control failed or was forgotten.

"No, I should have taken care of it and I didn't. It's not even a little bit your fault," he assured her, reaching out to brush her hair back from her temple. And then he smiled. "Well, maybe a little bit your fault," he amended, his eyes warm and appreciative, "for being so beautiful and sexy and making me lose my head in the first place."

"I'm sor—"

"Don't say it again," Gage warned, putting his finger against her lips. "And don't look so tragic." He removed his finger, replacing its pressure with that of a quick kiss. "There's probably nothing to worry about." He waited a moment but she didn't respond. "Is there?"

She continued to stare up at him.

"Is it a safe time of the month for you?"

"Oh, that. Yes, it is. That is, I think so . . . no, no, I'm sure it is," she amended quickly, seeing the frown of concern beginning to form between his brows. "It's safe," she lied, although, in reality, she had no idea if it was or not; a woman who hadn't had sex in five years had no reason to worry about the so-called safe time of the month. She wasn't even sure she knew when it was. "Perfectly safe."

"Nothing's perfectly safe," Gage said, cynicism coloring his voice, "so we'll have to settle for probably safe for now." He levered himself off her body and propped up on an elbow beside her. "When will you know for sure?"

"A few days. Or a week, maybe," she answered, trying to gauge from his expression if she'd guessed it right. Apparently she had, because his frown cleared. "Not long."

He gave her a rueful little grin. "Unless you're waiting to find out if the rabbit's going to die."

"Do rabbits still die that way?" she asked, trying to treat it lightly, trying to pretend, for his sake—and her own—that what they were discussing wasn't a matter of any great importance.

Gage lifted one broad shoulder in a shrug. "Probably not," he replied. "I think it's all done with test tubes now. Surrogate rabbits." His smile faded. "You'll let me know when you're sure, won't you?" he said seriously. "Either way. If you're . . ." he hesitated, as if he found the word hard to say ". . . pregnant, we'll find a way to deal with it."

"Yes, of course I'll let you know," she answered, lying for the second time in as many minutes. She already knew she'd only tell him if it was news he wanted to hear, because he probably wouldn't hear her, anyway, if she told him anything else. Bobby Clay hadn't. According to her mother, her father hadn't, either. Men never wanted to hear about the unintended consequences of their passion.

"So—" He reached out and circled a nimble finger around the rosy crest of her breast. He told himself he was only trying to distract both of them from the disquieting subject at hand, but it was only half the truth. The other half of it was that he wanted her again—as fiercely as if he hadn't already lost himself in her twice. "Why don't we test one of those Trojans I brought with me?" he suggested, giving her a fervent look. "Be a shame to waste all of them."

Tara caught her hand in his. "It's late."

"Not that late."

"And I have an early call in the morning."

"I know." He wriggled his fingers under her restraining hand, tickling the sensitive outer curve of her breast. "We both do."

"But only one of us has to be in front of the camera, looking as if she had a good night's sleep the night before."

"We could make it a quickie."

She hesitated, torn between the passion he so easily roused in her and the fear of what havoc that passion had already wrought in her life. "How quick?"

"Well . . . not *too* quick," he said, seeing the heat building in her eyes. He slipped his hand out from under hers and ran his fingertip around the areola of her other breast, watching intently as the nipple puckered and came to rigid attention. "But quick enough." He looked up at her and gave her a smile that promised untold delights if she would just trust herself to him one more time. "You could be asleep by ten."

Passion won out. It was new and exciting, and all too fleeting to deny. The fear would still be there tomorrow. And the damage—if damage there was—had already been done. Denying herself the joy he could give her wouldn't change what had already happened. "Make it ten-thirty," she said, reaching up to wrap her arms around his neck.

The loving was slow this time, lingering and sweet, and so deliciously languorous that she wasn't asleep by ten, as he'd promised, or even ten-thirty. Gage drew the experience out, kissing and caressing every sensitive place on her body—and some she hadn't known were sensitive at all.

He made a concerted effort to sate himself on her luscious flesh. Making sure no pleasure points were missed or neglected, he nuzzled the curve of her neck and the insides of her elbows and the backs of her knees. He nibbled on her fingers and toes and all the sweet delicacies in between. He whispered to her—accolades to her beauty and responsiveness and hot, torrid words that told her what he was doing and what he was going to do and how it would make them both feel when he did it.

Gently but inexorably he encouraged her to respond in kind, knowing that having her touch him would go a long way toward alleviating the intensity of his need.

Thus subtly persuaded, Tara found herself eager to experience the textures and tastes of a male body, found herself breathless to discover everything that made the man in her arms so excitingly different from herself—and from every other man she'd ever known.

She touched him hesitantly at first and then with more confidence as she became aware of how powerfully her slightest caress affected him. The whisper of her fingertips across the angular planes of his face made him sigh. The slightest touch on his chest made his tiny male nipples contract and his heart beat faster. The merest feathering stroke across his hard, flat belly made him quiver with the need for more. The clasp of her fingers around his erection made him arch and moan and call her name in a low, ragged voice. And when, at last, it came time to unroll the condom onto his hard length, she insisted on helping, delighting in the knowledge that she had brought him to such a forceful state of arousal, rather than being dismayed by it as she had always been in the past.

He mounted her then, parting her soft thighs with his hard hairy ones, filling her slowly, moving in her with deep, measured strokes until she arched and cried out, her voluptuous body sweat sheened and trembling beneath him. His thrusts became driving and insistent as she came apart in his arms. His muscles bunched and quivering, his breathing labored, he strove to push them both to the shuddering edge of delirium—and over.

"I'm not as young as I used to be," he said when he finally lay—wrung out, replete and panting—beside her on the tumbled bed. "So it takes a little longer the third time."

Tara sighed and stretched beside him, sinuous as a cat, her mind and body full to overflowing with the sensual satisfaction of a woman well-and-thoroughly loved, her vulnerable heart weaving girlish, romantic dreams out of the splendor of their loving. "Do I look like I mind?" she purred.

He turned his head on the pillow. "No," he responded, letting his gaze wander from her glowing face to the full, flushed globes of her breasts, to the sleek skin of her belly and back again. "You look like a woman who's been very thoroughly..."

She lifted an eyebrow, daring him to say it.

". . . enjoyed," he finished with a teasing grin.

Tara brought her arms back down to her sides and rolled over to face him. She tucked one hand beneath her cheek—like a child settling down to sleep, he thought—and smiled shyly. "I enjoyed it, too," she said simply. "Very much. It was . . ." she sighed, managing, somehow, to give him that enticing little sideways glance of hers even though he could have sworn she was looking directly at him ". . . wonderful. *You* were wonderful."

Gage felt his heart swell with some powerful emotion. Pride, he decided quickly, because that was less scary than whatever else it might be. Just plain, old-fashioned, undoubtedly chauvinistic, entirely masculine pride at having put that look of melting satisfaction on Tara Channing's exquisite face. That was all it could be. All he'd let it be.

"I don't know how to describe it," Tara went on in a dreamy, far-away voice. She lifted her hand, reaching out to touch him, trying wordlessly to express the wonder and gratitude she felt. "It was the most—"

"Please," Gage interrupted, his voice deliberately offhand, almost indifferent, in a panicked effort to stop her before she said something she'd regret. Something *he'd* regret. "If you say any more, I'll blush."

Tara's expression cooled in an instant. Her fingers, as they lifted the damp hair off his forehead, were suddenly more casual than tender. Her silly dreams faded. "A Kingston—blush?" She gave his hair a casual flick before dropping her hand to the mattress between them. "I'd like to get that on film."

"Film?"

"There are people who'd pay good money to see it," she said flippantly, instinctively knowing the best way to put him at a distance. "And pay well." She yawned extravagantly and glanced over at the small enameled clock on the nightstand before he could reply to her comment. "Goodness, it's after eleven." She reached down to find the blankets that were tangled around their feet and pulled them up over her bare shoulders, snuggling under them as if the temperature of the room were the only reason for her sudden chill. "It's been fun," she said, giving him a cool, insouciant look that belied and belittled the heated hours they'd just spent in each other's arms, "but I really have to get my beauty sleep." She yawned again. "Lock the door on your way out, would you?" she added, and closed her eyes.

She lay very still for the next few moments, waiting to see what he would do, hoping he would do ... something. And then the mattress shifted as he got off the bed, and she heard the whisper and slide of his clothes as he got into them, the slither and scrape of his leather belt and shoes as he rescued them from where they had fallen.

She waited until she heard the door to her trailer close before she rolled onto her back and opened her eyes to stare, dry-eyed and unseeing, at the ceiling over her bed.

GAGE CLOSED THE DOOR to her trailer with exaggerated care, fighting the urge to slam it hard enough to break the little frosted glass window in its upper half. He'd been used! Used and then summarily dismissed, like some gigolo summoned to bed for a night's entertainment, only to be kicked back out into the cold when the fun was over.

Just who in the hell did she think she was, anyway? Kicking *him* out of *her* bed! And after he'd given her his all, too! After he'd tied himself up in knots like some callow boy with his first crush. Didn't it count that he'd tried to be a gentleman? Didn't it mean *anything* to her that he'd wooed her like a bride once he had her in his arms, going out of his way to make it as good for her as he could? It'd taken a superhuman effort to hold himself back from falling on her in a frenzy of lust the minute he had her alone. A *superhuman* effort. But had she appreciated his restraint? Hell, no! He might as well have satisfied himself right at the start, and never mind making sure she enjoyed it, too, if that's all the thanks he was going to get!

Damn, he wanted to hit something!

Or find a honky-tonk with a jukebox full of George Jones songs and get stinking drunk.

And then hit something.

Or someone.

If it wasn't sixty miles to the nearest town—though calling the one-street burg a town was being generous—he might appropriate one of the company vehicles and do just that. But it was sixty miles. And the roads were icy. And if he got in a bare-knuckle brawl in a hick town he'd probably end up in jail. Then Hans would have apoplexy, which would really throw a monkey wrench into the shooting schedule. His mother would descend on the set—subzero temperatures be damned—demanding explanations, and he'd have to explain himself to her. And no one in his right mind wanted to have to explain to Elise Gage why one of her movies had gone over budget and her elder son had ended up in jail. Especially if the someone doing the explaining was responsible for both problems.

So Elise's elder son stomped around under the bright Montana stars in the biting cold, swearing and kicking at shadows, until he'd calmed down enough to open the door to his trailer without tearing it off its hinges. If Pierce was asleep, Gage didn't want to wake him; he wasn't in the mood to listen to any of his brother's smart-ass remarks.

Pierce, unfortunately, was very much awake.

He lay stretched out on the sofa, a crystal snifter on the low table beside him, a vintage Abbott and Costello video flickering, sans sound, on the television screen. A pair of glasses were perched on the end of his classic nose as he studied the thick script propped up on his chest. He raised his eyes in mild surprise as the door opened. "I didn't expect you back tonight."

"And I didn't expect you to still be up."

"Claire expressed this—" he said in explanation, indicating the script he was holding "—this afternoon. Said she thought it would be perfect for my next project."

"Will it?"

"Has our baby sister ever been wrong?"

"Not about the business." Gage shrugged out of his jacket and threw it across the opposite end of the sofa from where his brother lay. It covered Pierce's feet. "You finished with that?" Gage asked, gesturing toward the snifter.

"Help yourself."

Gage picked up the glass and drained it in one gulp.

"That's fifty-year-old Armagnac," Pierce said mildly.

"Got any more?"

"On the bar." Pierce nodded toward the rosewood cabinet against the opposite wall. "But if you're going to drink it without tasting it, I'd recommend the jug wine in the refrigerator instead."

Gage ignored him and poured a double shot of the rich amber liquid into a snifter.

Pierce pulled his feet out from under Gage's jacket and put them on the floor. He reached for the remote control and depressed the Power button, shutting off the video. "You want to talk about it?" he asked, setting the script and his reading glasses down on the coffee table.

Gage threw himself into a chair. "No," he snarled and lifted the crystal snifter to his lips for a healthy swallow.

Pierce waited.

Gage scowled into his drink.

Pierce waited some more.

"She kicked me out."

"Before or after?" Pierce asked, wondering if Gage had spent his evening at the floating poker game that was always going on in one or other of the trailers.

Gage lifted the snifter to his lips. "After," he mumbled into the glass.

"Were you that bad?"

"No." He stopped scowling at his drink to scowl at his brother. "Things were going great. We'd just—" He hesitated, unwilling to reveal any of the intimate details. *It was wonderful*, she'd said, with that soft dreamy look on her face. *You were wonderful.* "Things were going great," he repeated, looking down into his glass as he swirled Armagnac up the sides. "And then she said it had been fun but she needed to get her beauty sleep. She actually had the nerve to ask me to lock the door on my way out," he said indignantly. "Like I was some guy she'd picked up for the night but didn't want hanging around in the morning."

Pierce hid a smile. "So what's the problem?"

Gage looked up at his brother, incredulity evident in his expression.

"Isn't that exactly the kind of relationship you wanted with her?" Pierce said reasonably. "No strings. No commitments."

"Well, yeah, but . . ."

"But you wanted to be the one to set the boundaries and lay out the ground rules," Pierce said shrewdly. "And you're mad now because she beat you to it."

"I'm not mad."

"What, then?"

Gage was silent for a moment. Was Pierce right? Was that all it was? Just pure contrary cussedness because she'd been the one to make the rules? "Hell, I don't know," he said irritably. "I guess maybe you're right."

He hoped his brother was right; it didn't bear thinking about if he wasn't. If this feeling churning around inside him was something more than a product of sex and anger and affronted male pride he was in big trouble. Very big trouble. Worse than he'd ever been in with Alyssa. Gage tossed off the rest of his drink and stood. "I'm going to bed," he said gruffly, and slammed the glass down on the table.

Pierce stared after him with a little half smile on his handsome face and a lot of hope in his heart.

Tara Channing was just exactly what his older brother needed to break down the wall he'd built around his heart after Alyssa got through with him—*if* he could be made to see it before it was too late.

8

TARA AND GAGE WERE excruciatingly polite to each other the next morning, in the way only two people who have been intimate and then have doubts about it can be. Like two teenagers, unsure of each other's feelings and their own, each surreptitiously watched the other with avid interest while studiously avoiding any situation that would put them in proximity of each other. While carefully pretending not to care, each of them knew, every minute, exactly where the other one was. And who they were talking to. And what they were doing.

Does she have to stand so damn close to Hans while he explains what he wants her to do?

Does he have to hang his arm around that woman's neck to discuss camera angles?

Does she have to smile at every man as if he were the only man on earth?

Does he have to look at every woman as if he wonders what she'd be like in bed?

Didn't last night mean anything?!

"Quit acting like an ass and go talk to her," Pierce advised his brother after about twenty minutes of observing this adolescent behavior from afar. "You know you want to." He paused for a telling fraction of a second. "Everyone else knows you want to, too."

Gage's answer was a bad-tempered scowl and an anatomically impossible suggestion.

Pierce grinned and wandered away to spread mischief elsewhere. "You two aren't fooling anybody with this little charade, you know," he said to Tara a moment later. "Except maybe yourselves."

Tara's reply was more temperate than Gage's had been. "I beg your pardon?" she said, staring down into her steaming mug of tea as if she had absolutely no idea what he could possibly be talking about.

"I think you hurt his feelings last night when you threw him out of your bed."

That brought her head up. "*I* hurt *his* feelings—" she began indignantly. A burst of masculine laughter had her teeth snapping together and her eyes turning involuntarily toward the source of the sound. "He certainly looks like his feelings are hurt," she said sarcastically, watching Gage enjoy himself with another woman. She shifted her gaze back to Pierce and glared at him. "And I didn't throw him out of my bed."

"No?"

"No. He left of his own free will." Her jaw clenched. Her fingers tightened around the heavy mug in her hands. "He couldn't *wait* to leave."

"One of you has sure got this whole thing wrong. Or both of you are—"

"Tara, my dear, are you ready to run through it?"

"Certainly, Hans." She handed Pierce her mug of tea. "Keep this warm for me, will you, sweetie?" she said loudly, giving him a lingering smile and one of those beguiling looks from under her lashes.

Pierce didn't need to be told that Gage was watching them; he could feel his brother's gaze boring into the back of his head. "I'll be right here, waiting for you, darling," he said caressingly, loud enough for his brother to hear.

Behind him, Gage snarled.

"Places everybody," yelled the A.D. "We're gonna run through it."

"It" was Tara's big action scene, with five cameras set up to film Yelena's panicked and stealthy flight through the alleyways from the grimy back window of a garage where she'd been spying on her brother and his co-conspirators. Hans had directed that one camera be hoisted up on a crane for a long shot of the action. Two others were placed for strategic close-ups as she rounded corners or flattened herself against the side of a building. The remaining two cameras were on dollies, one in front of Tara, moving backward as she advanced, the other, with Gage behind the lens, tracking along beside her. Each camera was equipped with a special day-for-night filter to simulate the darkness of late night, and different cuts from each would eventually be combined into one apparently seamless whole when the film was edited.

They rehearsed it four times to get the blocking and camera angles right. Four times, Tara darted away from her place by the window as if she feared she'd been detected. Four times, she stumbled and slipped down frozen alleyways and between the false fronts of buildings to avoid detection. Four times, she sprinted, her shawl flying off of her head to expose her to the biting cold as she sprinted across an open space to the small frame building that represented the house she shared with her fictional brother. Her nose and cheeks were wind-chapped and pink, her fingers stiff with cold, the hem of her heavy coat wet and clammy with snow by the time Hans was finally satisfied with the sequence and timing of the action.

She could have used a stand-in for all this, Gage thought sourly, watching her through the lens of his camera. But no, she had to show everyone what a little trouper she was by refusing to send her double out into the cold for the run-throughs. "It isn't as if it's danger-ous, or anything," she'd said when Hans had offered her the option. Still determined not to give in to his feel-ings—any feelings—for her, Gage tried not to admire her for being so damned cheerful and uncomplaining no matter how many times Hans asked her to do it over. But it was hard not to be impressed, especially when his own fingers, left bare to better operate the camera, were numb and everyone else was grumbling about the cold and the snow and the repeated run-throughs.

"All right," Hans said finally, after Tara had had her makeup renewed and had exchanged her damp, spat-tered coat for another one exactly like it. "Let's roll film on this one." He turned to Tara where she stood with her hands wrapped around another warming mug of tea. "Take it all the way from the beginning to the end without stopping," he instructed her. "I want an un-broken master shot of the whole scene, then we'll break it down by sections."

Tara nodded and handed her cup to a waiting grip in exchange for her shawl, which had been hung to warm in front of a heater. "Bless you, Arlo," she said, smiling

at the young man who handed it to her. Then, looking
into a mirror held by a woman from Wardrobe, she
wrapped the shawl around her head and shoulders,
tucking in her hair so not a strand showed. Her face,
seemingly bare of makeup and framed by the thick
black wool of the shawl, had the stark purity of a clois-
tered, unworldly nun.

Until she smiled, Gage thought, watching as she
thanked the burly grip who gave her a hand onto the
rickety wooden box placed under the window. When
she smiled like that she looked like an angel who could
tempt a saint to sin. Repeatedly.

"Roll film," Hans said. "And . . . action."

Moving stealthily, Tara gripped the windowsill for
balance and pulled herself up on tiptoe. She put her face
close to the glass, peering in as if straining to see. Her
lovely brow was furrowed as if she were also straining
to hear what was supposedly being said. A sixth camera inside captured every nuance of her expression.

"Now," Hans said, signaling that someone had detected her presence.

Tara gasped and pulled back, ducking down as if she
feared she'd been seen. Her fingers slipped from the sill
and she tottered backward, off the wooden box. She
caught herself, managing to stay upright, but it fell
over, toppling to its side in the snow with a muffled
thud. She froze, her frightened gaze going to the door
for a long, agonized moment, and then she turned and
fled down the alley as if all the hounds of hell were
slobbering at her heels. She moved as quickly as she
dared, her progress hindered by the frozen, snow-
packed ground, icy in spots, and the frantic need to be

as quiet as possible. Once she flattened herself against the side of a building, pulling up a corner of her shawl to shield her face. A moment later, she shrank back into the shadows of a doorway and sank her teeth into her bottom lip, as if holding back a whimper of fear. Then she sighed—a deep sound of relief at danger momentarily averted—and sprinted away again. Down another narrow street she went, breathing hard now. Her shawl slipped from her head, falling around her shoulders, freeing the wild tangle of her hair so that it sailed behind her like a banner. The camera moving away in front of her recorded the sheer terror on her face, the camera tracking at her side focused on the subdued frenzy of her movements.

And then she slipped, coming down hard on the frozen ground as her feet shot out from under her. She lay there for a second or two, obviously dazed by the force of the fall.

"No," Hans said sharply, throwing out an arm to stop Gage as he instinctively moved away from his camera to go to her.

Gage growled, low in his throat, and started to shake the director off, but Tara, still totally in character, was already pushing herself to her feet.

She finished the dash to safety, her right hand pressed against her side as if it hurt her, her posture hunched as she ran. The camera in front of her turned to follow her progress, shooting her from the back now as she fled. She hobbled up to the door of the house and threw it open, all but falling through it as she stumbled over the threshold. It slammed shut behind her with a final, resounding thud.

There was a moment's silence. "Cut and print," Hans said, his voice rich with satisfaction in the cold Montana air because they'd somehow gotten the scene in one take.

They waited a moment more, then two, for Tara to come out of the building. It was bare and cold inside, used only for its exterior, no place one would want to linger, even for a moment.

And then Gage swore and was off his dolly cart and dashing across the frozen ground. Several members of the crew started to rush after him.

"Wait," Pierce said, halting them. A smile turned up the corners of his mouth, exposing the dimple in his lean cheek. "Let's see what happens if we leave them alone for a minute."

"ARE YOU ALL RIGHT?" Gage demanded, crashing through the door after her. "Tara, damn it," he roared, unable to see very far into the interior of the small building. After the brilliant sunlight shining on the snow outside, it appeared almost pitch-dark inside. "Where are you?"

"I'm right—" she took a deep breath "—here."

He turned his head toward the sound of her voice and saw a shadowy form against the far wall. It appeared as if she were leaning on it, hunched over against some agonizing pain. He reached her in two strides and put his hands out to touch her. "Where does it hurt?" he asked, running his hands down her shoulders and arms.

"Nowhere," she said, still breathing heavily. "It doesn't hurt anywhere. I'm just—" she stopped, gasping, as his hands moved down her legs.

"Damn it, I knew it. You've hurt yourself." He crossed back to the door for a second. "She's going to need a doctor," he yelled, then swung around and lifted her into his arms.

"Gage, for heaven's sake. I'm not hurt, I'm just—"

"Be quiet, now," he soothed, carrying her through the doorway. "Just hang on. We'll have you fixed up in no time."

"Gage, I'm—"

"Tara, my dear, I had no idea you'd really hurt yourself." Hans looked worried and guilt-stricken. "I would have stopped filming if I'd known," he assured her.

"I'm *not* hurt," she said again, looking over Gage's shoulder at the director's face as her rescuer marched through the crowd toward her trailer. "I'm fine. Pierce, tell them," she said, appealing to the one person who might be able to get through to the madman who held her in his arms. "I'm just a little out of breath, is all. From the run. I didn't hurt myself when I fell. I was acting. *Tell him.*"

Pierce smiled and shrugged, lifting his hands, palms up, in a helpless gesture as if to say, *No one can tell him anything.*

"Oh, for heaven's sake." She said again as Gage shifted his hold on her to open her trailer door. "This is totally ridiculous. I'm not hurt."

Still ignoring her protests, he turned sideways and shouldered his way into the trailer, careful not to knock or nudge her against the metal doorframe.

"No doctors," she said to the faces gathered outside her door. "I don't need a doc—"

The door shut on her words, pulled closed from the outside by the interfering hand of Pierce Kingston.

"Gage, really, I'm fine," Tara said as he set her gently on the edge of the bed and knelt in front of her. He tossed his sheepskin jacket to the floor and reached out to unwind the shawl from around her throat and shoulders. "Gage." She slapped at his hands. "Will you stop that, please, and listen to me? I'm fine. Fine, you know? As in not hurt. As in uninjured." She curled her fingers into the soft wool and held on, trying to keep him from taking it. "As in undamaged and unharmed. As in, I was only out of breath from the run and I'm fine."

His fingers stilled on the shawl. "Humor me," he said, low, without quite meeting her eyes.

"Why should I?" The words were pouty, demanding answers and explanations. And reassurance.

He looked up at her then, his amber eyes filled with a strange, unnerving light. "Because you scared me half to death," he said, letting go of her shawl to show her his hands. They were trembling. "And I want to see for myself that you're all right."

"Why?" she said softly.

"Why do I want to see for myself?" he asked, hoping to avoid what he knew was the real question.

She shook her head. "Why did seeing me fall make your hands tremble?"

"I don't know."

"Don't you?"

"No, damn it, I don't!" he burst out, telling the truth as he knew it. "I only know that I need to see for myself, with my own eyes, that you're all right."

"And then what?"

There was a long, tense silence as they stared at each other, two pairs of eyes filled with needs and fears, uncertainty and longing. "And then I want to make love to you until neither of us can see anything but each other."

Tara thought about it as she sat there, unable to tear her gaze away from his. Thought about it hard. No man had ever cared enough to tremble with fear for her. Nor, until last night, had anyone trembled in true passion, either. It wasn't what she had hoped to hear when she asked her question but it was, she realized, enough to make her cast her doubts aside. For now, it was more than enough.

"All right," she said, and let go of the shawl.

Wordlessly, almost frantically, Gage undressed her. There was none of the finesse of the night before. No lingering caresses or prolonged kisses. No sweet wooing of her senses to make her ready. He simply peeled her out of her clothes as fast as possible, ran his hands over her to make sure she'd taken no serious hurt and then reached for the zipper on his jeans. Tumbling her backward on the satin-covered bed, he pushed the denim down his hips. His entry was so swift and hard, his movements within her so fierce, that it should have hurt. But it didn't. From the moment she'd looked down at his hands and seen them trembling, she'd been ready to receive him. To welcome him.

With a wordless cry, she wrapped her strong slim legs around his hips and met his wild thrusts with a wildness of her own, reveling in his rampant unrestrained possession of her. She could feel the scrape of his denim jeans against the insides of her soft thighs and the buttons of his chambray shirt rubbing against her belly and breasts and the sweet silkiness of his hair against her neck and cheek. She could hear the muted thud of flesh against willing flesh, and his harsh labored breathing and her own feral little cries of exultant need. And then he arched in her arms, his hips pressing down, his whole big body stiffening and straining against her, his breath escaping in a long, low groan of triumphant satisfaction. His climax triggered Tara's and she stiffened in turn, her legs locked tight around him, her fingers clutching at his hair to hold him close as she bit down on her bottom lip to stifle her own cry of ecstasy.

They lay quietly for a few moments as their mutual shuddering subsided, both of them stunned and panting, fighting to make sense out of what had just happened. And then Gage spoke, his words warm against the damp curve of her neck.

"Don't ever, *ever* do that to me again," he ordered softly.

"No," Tara said, just as softly. "I won't."

He lifted his head. "I mean it," he said sternly, staring down at her. He knew he wasn't making sense, that his reaction was all out of proportion with what had happened, but it didn't seem to make any difference. Some part of his mind put it down to an unusual and highly developed sense of possession that screamed *mine!* whenever he looked at her. Another, even more primitive part wanted to make absolutely sure that his possession was unquestioned and complete. He moved his hands up to her head and threaded his fingers through the glorious tangle of her sun-kissed hair.

Cupping her skull in his wide palms, he pushed her chin up with his thumbs so that her throat was arched and vulnerable. "It nearly made my heart stop," he said, and bent his head.

He pressed his lips to the base of her neck in a hot, openmouthed kiss that spoke of both ownership and apology. It was a rich kiss, a deep, lingering, sucking kiss that asked for forgiveness for his earlier swift possession of her, while declaring his right to do so again.

Tara knew she'd be marked when he lifted his head but she couldn't find it in herself to care. She moaned instead, in submission and compliance, feeling gloriously female and deliciously, passionately desired. And when he lifted his head, she raised hers, too, and bit him on the shoulder, hard enough to leave teeth marks that would last awhile.

He grunted in pleasure and then, helplessly, tenderly, began their lovemaking all over again.

THEY MADE LOVE TWICE MORE that afternoon, stopping once to sleep for a short time before rousing to each other again. Absorbed in heated sensation and erotic excess, they blithely consigned the world outside to oblivion until the time came when Gage was forced to reach for the switch on the crystal lamp by the bed to chase away the lengthening shadows at the end of the winter's day.

"So much for discretion," he said, dropping a little kiss onto the tip of Tara's nose as he settled back down beside her.

"Discretion?" she murmured, snuggling against him with the contentment of a kitten in familiar hands.

"It's after four o'clock."

"So?"

"So, we've been in this trailer since, oh, maybe one o'clock this afternoon."

Tara came up on her elbow, lifting her head to look at him with an expression of alarm in her aquamarine eyes.

"With Pierce and Hans and everybody waiting around for us to come out," he added, grinning as her expression of alarm turned to one of horrified dismay.

"Oh, my God," she murmured.

"They probably had to shut down production for the day," Gage went on in a teasing tone. "I can just imagine what Hans will have to say to that."

Tara dropped her forehead onto his chest. "Oh, my God," she repeated.

"And then there's my mother's reaction when she sees the daily production reports. She's planning on releasing *The Promise* next Christmas and she's gonna hate it if anything screws up her plans."

Tara made a strangled noise and rolled her forehead against his chest, speechless at the very thought.

"Come on, now, sweetheart," he teased, trying to work his hand under her chin so he could make her look up at him. "It's not that bad."

"Not that bad..." Tara let him raise her head, revealing a face crimson with embarrassment. "How can you say it's not that bad? We've stopped production on a major movie to... to..."

His grin widened. "It's not the first time it's ever happened."

"It's the first time it's happened to me!" she wailed, and buried her face in his chest again.

"It is?"

Tara went very still for a moment, and then she jerked out of his arms and sat up, snatching at a sheet to cover herself.

"Hey, wait a minute," Gage said, closing the fingers of one hand around her arm before she could fling herself off the bed. "I was just kidding."

She gave him a hard-eyed look. "Were you?"

"Yes, damn it, I was," he said, wondering if he was telling the whole truth. On a conscious level, he *had* been just kidding, joking to tease her out of her seriousness. On an unconscious level he wasn't quite sure. Deep inside of him there was that old-fashioned, unenlightened, testosterone-soaked part of his brain that couldn't help but wonder how many men had whiled away entire days in her bed. He knew it wasn't fair, that it wasn't any of his business, that—given the fleeting nature of their relationship—he didn't really want to make it his business but, still, he wondered. And the old jealousy, the battered masculine pride, pricked at him to do something about it.

He tried to ignore it.

"Let go of me," Tara demanded then, straining against his hold.

"Let's not fight again," he said cajolingly, refusing to let go. He rubbed his forefinger up and down her arm. "The last thing I want to do is fight with you."

She gave him a lethal, narrow-eyed look that said, quite plainly, that she didn't particularly care what he wanted.

"I said I was only kidding."

Her expression didn't change. "I don't believe you."

All cajolery fled. "Are you calling me a liar?"

"Isn't that what you're calling me? A liar? And worse."

"I'm not calling you anything. I— Oh, hell!" He let go of her arm and sat up, lifting both hands to run them through his disordered hair. "I don't know what I'm doing around you, let alone what I'm saying. I just—"

"You just what?"

"I just look at you and I go crazy, that's 'just what,'" he said belligerently.

"And it's all my fault, too, I suppose?"

"Yes. No. Damn it!" One fist hit the bed in impotent fury. "How the hell am I supposed to know? You're the one with the reputation for this sort of thing."

She stared back at him for a heartbeat or two, silently, sadly. There was no way to respond to his remark in a way that would satisfy him; there was no way she was even going to try. No matter what she said, he would believe what he wanted to believe, and she had too much pride to try to change his mind. Besides, she'd stopped defending herself for all the things she hadn't done a long time ago.

She bent over and picked the black shawl up off the floor. "If that's what you think of me," she said, winding it around her body like a towel as she stood, "then there's nothing more to say, is there?"

"Tara. Damn it, Tara, wait." He sprang up naked from the bed and grabbed her arm to stop her from walking into the bathroom and out of his life. "I didn't mean it the way it sounded."

She didn't struggle, didn't protest. She just stood there looking up at him, her hands clutching the black shawl together between her breasts, her beautiful face a complete blank.

"Look, I spoke without thinking, okay?" he said, transferring his grip to her shoulders, turning her so that she was facing him directly. "And I'm sorry."

The blank look didn't change.

"I just said the first stupid thing that came into my head, but it didn't mean anything. *I* didn't mean anything."

Still no response.

"All right, damn it, I was crazy with jealousy," he admitted, getting desperate now at her lack of response. "Thinking about all the other men that've been in your life made me a little nuts and I...I..." He floundered, knowing whatever he said was only going to get him in deeper.

"I suppose this means you've been celibate since your divorce," Tara said acidly.

Gage sighed. "No, I haven't. And you're absolutely right," he said, tacitly admitting the truth implied by her sarcastic words. "I have no right to question your past when my own has been less than admirable."

"You have no right to question my past at all."

"No, you're right there, too," he agreed, knowing, deep down, that she was. "I don't. And I'm sorry I even presumed to try."

"Apology accepted," Tara said tonelessly. "Now, let me go, please."

"Can't we talk about this?"

"There's nothing to talk about," she said wearily.

"Yes, there is, damn it!" He gentled both his hands and his tone as she shrank back in his hold. "Yes, there is," he said again, more moderately. "But not here. Here there are too many... listen, what do you say we get away from this place for a while? Out of this trailer," he suggested. "We could take one of the Jeeps and drive into town. Find a quiet little restaurant and talk over dinner." He let go of her shoulders as he spoke, letting her make the decision without coercion from him. "What do you say, Tara?" he asked with a humility completely foreign to him. "Shall we find some neutral ground and talk this out?"

For a minute he didn't think she was going to agree, then slowly, she nodded.

Relief flooded through him. "Good," he said, afraid to stop to consider why he was so relieved. "That's good." He bent over, scooped his clothes up off the floor and began pulling them on. "I'll go round up some transportation while you get dressed."

THE RESTAURANT they found was small and definitely quiet, with every booth but the one they took empty and only a handful of customers at the bar.

"Definitely not Spagos," Gage commented after they'd given their drink orders to the uniformed waitress.

"No," Tara agreed, looking around her. "In fact, it kind of reminds me of where I grew up."

"Where's that?"

"Clayville, Texas. It's a little town in the Panhandle." She glanced around the small rough-hewn restaurant, her gaze taking in the worn genuine imitation red leather seating, the open rafters above their heads, the initials scratched on the surface of the table and carved into the wooden sides of the booth, the soft lights flashing on the jukebox by the bar. There wasn't a lot of fondness in her expression. "There was a place just like this at the edge of town. Quiet as a tomb during the week, but on Saturday nights all the cowboys came in to howl."

"Did you howl there, too?"

"Me?" She looked up from the red-and-white checked paper napkin she was unwinding from around the silverware. "No, I didn't do any howling at the Roundup."

"Then how do you know what it was like?"

"My mother was a waitress there."

"And your father? Was he one of the cowboys who came in to howl?"

"No." She looked down, uncomfortable with the direction the conversation had taken, and spread the napkin across her lap.

"What did he—"

"Here's your drinks, folks," the waitress said as she set two frosty beer mugs down on the table in front of them. "Now—" she slipped her order pad and pencil out of the pocket of her apron "—you ready to order yet?" She wet the tip of the pencil with her tongue and waited expectantly. "The chicken-fried steak is the best thing on the menu," she said when neither of them offered a selection.

Gage cocked an eyebrow at his dinner companion. "Chicken-fried steak?"

"Beefsteak pounded thin, dredged in flour and fried like chicken. Served with—" Tara looked up at the waitress "—mashed potatoes and country gravy?"

"Yep," she confirmed, "and green beans cooked in pot likker and bacon grease, with homemade biscuits and honey on the side."

"Sold," Gage said, and handed his menu to the waitress.

Tara sighed. "Make it two," she said, relinquishing her own menu. She looked back at Gage after the waitress had gone to turn in their orders. "That's an extra five miles on the bicycle tomorrow." She, smiled. "I hope it's worth it."

Gage smiled back at her. "Is it usually?"

"Is what usually?" Tara asked absently, suddenly entranced by the way his eyes crinkled up at the corners when he smiled at her.

"The chicken-fried steak, is it . . ."

His voice trailed off as he caught the look in her eyes and they sat there, staring at each other over the scarred red linoleum table with the soft golden light from the nubby white glass candle holder flickering on their faces. A coin tumbled through the jukebox in the silence, the mechanical arm whirred softly, dropping a record into place, and Patsy Cline began to sing "Crazy."

And still they stared.

Am I crazy? Tara wondered, as the heartbreaking words of the old country standard washed over her. *Crazy to be here? Crazy to be falling in love? Crazy to be in love?* Like the song said, he was going to love her, and leave her crying. She knew it, and yet here she sat, practically inviting it to happen. *I am crazy*, she thought, staring at him with her aching heart in her eyes.

"Tara?" Gage said hesitantly. There was something in those beautiful eyes of hers. Something that called to a place deep inside him. "Tara, I—"

"No," she cut in, reaching across the table to touch her fingertips to his lips. "Not yet. Let's not talk about it yet. Let's have our night out first. Let's just enjoy our dinner, and talk about our . . . relationship later." She smiled, deliberately banishing the mood that had nearly reduced her to tears a moment before. "Okay?"

Gage continued to stare at her for another heartbeat's worth of time. Half of him was glad she'd stopped him from saying . . . whatever it was he'd been going to say. Half of him still wanted to say it. Whatever it was. "Okay," he said softly. He reached up as he spoke, covering her hand with his, pressing her fingers to his lips for a brief moment. "We won't talk about our relationship now." He lowered their clasped hands to the middle of the table. "We'll pretend we don't even have a relationship, yet. That we're . . ." He paused, thinking. "That we're on our first date. We'll talk about whatever it is people talk about then." He gave her a quizzical, comical look. "What do people talk about on first dates?"

"Themselves, mostly," Tara said wryly, thinking of all the men she'd been on first dates with.

"Okay," Gage agreed. "Tell me about yourself."

"Your life's much more interesting than mine."

Gage shook his head. "You first." He clasped her hand more comfortably in his. "Tell me all about Tara Channing."

"What do you want to know?" she asked cautiously.

"Oh, anything." *Everything*, he thought. *I want to know every little detail of how you got to be the woman you are.* "Tell me how you got from Clayville, Texas, to Hollywood, California."

Her smile was almost impish. "By bus."

"Details," he ordered sternly.

"Greyhound." She laughed softly at his expression. "It took five days."

"And at the end of those five days?"

"I got a job working as a waitress in a little café on Hollywood Boulevard. Not the greatest place in the world but the pay was okay," she said, neglecting to add that it had been barely enough to pay for a one-room apartment at a run-down residential hotel. "And my meals were included." Or she'd have had a tough time eating. "And then, two weeks later, just like Lana Turner at the soda fountain, I was discovered."

"That's a Hollywood myth, you know."

"What is?"

"That Lana Turner was discovered sitting at a soda fountain."

"Is it? Well," she said with a shrug, "it's true in my case. I went from being a waitress in a coffee shop one day to jiggling around in a bikini in some mindless beach movie the next."

"I'm sorry I missed that."

"I'm not."

"What did you do after that?"

"Well, let's see . . . I played a vampire bimbo in *Marauders of the Night*. It was my first speaking part."

Gage grinned at her obvious disdain for the role. "I'm afraid I missed that one, too." He unclasped his hand from hers and leaned back as the waitress set their meals down in front of them. "What else?"

"Say," the waitress said before Tara could answer. "Are you two from that movie company that's camped up the road at old man Bensenhurst's place?"

Gage and Tara glanced at each other, silently debating whether or not they could get away with a lie.

"Yes, we are," Gage confirmed, deciding they couldn't.

"Well, shoot! And you're sitting right here at my station. Are you somebody famous?"

"No," Gage denied without a flicker of guilt. "We're just a couple of working stiffs. The lady's an extra and I'm just a cameraman."

The waitress sighed, clearly disappointed in his answer. "Well, enjoy your dinner, anyway," she said, and headed back to the kitchen.

Gage and Tara burst into delighted laughter.

"*Just* a cameraman," Tara chided him, her eyes sparkling.

Their conversation stayed casual after that, bantering and playful as they sought to avoid the subject that was uppermost in both their minds.

"I saw you play one of Sam Malone's girlfriends on 'Cheers' a couple of years ago," Gage said. "I thought you did an excellent job with the part."

"Which part was that?" Tara shot back. "The jiggling or the cooing?"

"And there was that bit in 'Star Trek: The Next Generation.'"

"You mean the one where I got to say 'All the pleasures of our planet are yours for the asking' while wearing a blond wig and a loincloth?"

"Your delivery was superb."

Tara leveled a dour look at him. "My delivery?"

He grinned at her. "Among other things," he said, acknowledging her point. He forked a piece of steak into his mouth and chewed thoughtfully for a moment before continuing. "How about those two episodes you did on 'L.A. Law'? You can't say that was just cheesecake."

"No," Tara agreed. "It was still your basic bimbo role—with an evil, other-woman twist—but it wasn't cheesecake." She'd played a high-level administrative assistant who'd turned her boss in for inside trading in order to clear her way to the top of the corporate ladder. "And it led directly to my part as Jessica on 'As Time Goes By.'"

They ate in silence for a few moments.

"Did you always want to be a cinematographer?" Tara asked, reviewing their conversation.

"Always," Gage affirmed. "From the time I first set foot on a soundstage, I was fascinated with the cameras."

"And you never wanted to be in front of one?"

He shuddered theatrically. "Never. It's too much like exposing yourself as far as I'm concerned." He shot an apologetic smile across the table. "Not that I expect you to understand that. Pierce doesn't. He says acting is all about hiding who you are, not exposing yourself."

"Oh, I understand what you mean," Tara said fervently. "I've felt the same way myself in front of a camera, especially in the early days when I was exposing a lot more of myself than I wanted to."

And then, finally, over hot coffee and apple pie à la mode, they talked about what was really on their minds.

"My divorce was a disaster," Gage said, staring down at the pie in front of him as he pushed it around on the plate with his fork. "Hell—" he pushed the pie away and clasped his hands together on the table "—my entire marriage was a disaster. I found out later that Alyssa had been unfaithful almost from the beginning. She was beautiful and seductive and had the same air of innocence that you do. And I believed her. I believed *in* her. She fooled me for a long time." He looked up quickly, gauging her response, and then went back to staring at his clasped hands, struggling to find the right words to explain himself. "I refuse to be made a fool of that way again."

There was a long moment of silence. Gage sat, staring at his hands and waiting for her to say something. Tara sat and stared at his hands, too, remembering the way they'd trembled when he thought she was hurt, the way they'd trembled, later, in restrained passion and the gentle way he touched her in spite of it.

"And you think that's what I've been doing these last few days?" she asked. "Trying to make a fool of you?"

"No. But I think you could, anyway, without trying."

"Why?" she asked, mystified.

He looked up then, surprised that she didn't understand. "That's why. That air you have of not knowing the strength of your own appeal, when it's obvious that every man who looks at you wants you."

"But that's all hype. It's all—" she moved one hand in a fluttering motion in front of her "—all smoke and mirrors and window dressing. It's not me. I told you that before we ever started this. It's never been me."

Gage smiled grimly. "It's you."

Tara started to object, to profess her innocence, then decided against it. He would believe what he believed. And she wouldn't plead with anyone to think well of her. "So," she said. "Where do we go from here?"

"Where do you want to go?"

"I'd like to go back to before we were—" she made that little fluttering motion with her hand again, this time in the space between the two of them "—intimate, and try to be just friends. Because we could be friends," she added quickly, seeing the disagreement on his face. "Tonight proved that, if nothing else."

Gage shook his head. "I could never be just friends with you, Tara. I wouldn't want to be."

"Yes," she sighed, knowing deep down that he was right. "I know."

"If you're honest with yourself, you'll admit that you could never be just friends with me, either. Not now. Not after we've been—" he mimicked her gesture and her tone "—intimate. What's between us is too hot for mere friendship."

"I know that, too."

"So?"

"So we sever the relationship completely. Not friends. Not lovers. Just . . . colleagues. We should be able to manage that for the next three weeks, don't you think?" she said hopefully.

"No, I don't think," Gage said. "Especially when there's another option."

"Which is?"

"Friends *and* lovers. You said that tonight proved we could be friends, didn't you? Well, from this moment on, we forget the past. Yours and mine both. We put it all behind us and go on from here. No expectations, except for the here and now. No plans for the future. If it burns itself out in the next three weeks, then fine, we'll have had three great weeks together. If it lasts beyond that, then that's fine, too. We'll deal with it as it comes—one day at a time."

"And the jealousy?"

"Gone," he said, vowing to make it so. "I have no right to be jealous of your past and, as long as this lasts, I'll accept your word that I have no need to be jealous now. And you can expect the same from me," he added, before she could protest his choice of words. He held his hand out, palm up, across the table to her. "What do you say, Tara? Friends and lovers?"

Tara hesitated, torn, as the words to Patsy Cline's "Crazy" repeated themselves in her mind like a warning. She knew she was bound to be hurt by the arrangement he was suggesting; more than she already had been; more than she ever had before. *No expectations*, he'd said. *No plans for the future. One day at a time*. And when the relationship ended—in three weeks, or three months, or even three years—she was going to be left with a heart full of hurt and a mind full of memories. Glorious memories, perhaps, but just memories.

But if she said no now, if she turned him away, she wouldn't even have the memories.

"Yes," she said, and reached out across the table to put her hand in his. "Friends and lovers."

9

NO ONE WAS ILL-MANNERED enough to comment on their prolonged absence when they reported for work the next morning.

Except Pierce.

And Hans.

And three or four of the grips who'd placed bets on the exact nature of the activity going on inside the trailer the previous afternoon, as well as the number of actual encounters involved.

And the makeup girl, who had been so impressed with the love bite on Tara's neck that she told the entire crew about it.

And Arlo, who didn't actually say anything but looked at Gage with something akin to hero worship and blushed beet red every time Tara glanced his way.

"See," Gage teased her when Pierce congratulated them on their apparent stamina. "Nobody even noticed we were gone."

Tara groaned. "You think it's funny now," she warned, feeling compelled to point it out. "But the knowledge of how we spent yesterday afternoon isn't going to stop here. This whole thing is going to end up on the front page of next week's tabloids. You do know that, don't you?"

And Gage, who knew it very well but had avoided thinking of it until then, managed to say easily, "And who's going to tell the tabloids?"

"I don't know who tells them but somebody always does. With pictures and quotes from 'reliable sources' and lots of nasty innuendo."

"Well, look at it this way," said Pierce, who obviously wasn't finished tormenting them yet. "It'll be good publicity for the picture, and Hans and Mom will forgive you two for screwing—" He grinned wickedly. "Excuse me. Bad choice of words," he said when Tara blushed and Gage scowled. "Hans and Mother will forgive you for *messing* up the production schedule and putting us over budget."

As it turned out, the production schedule wasn't messed up at all.

"I'd blocked out the whole day to do that scene," Hans said when Tara tried to stammer her way through an apology. "But you were such a trooper—and that first take was so perfect—we didn't need the whole day. Of course, we could have been a little ahead of schedule if you and Gage had been on the job for the rest of the afternoon, but there was no real harm done, my dear," he assured her. "None at all."

He was a little more forthright and a lot less tactful with Gage. "If you two disappear like that again when there's still good shooting light left, I'm going to come pounding on the door myself and drag you out of bed, instead of politely waiting around for you to wear yourselves out, no matter what that brother of yours says. Am I making myself perfectly clear?"

"Perfectly," Gage said shortly, reining in his temper because he knew he deserved the rebuke.

"Well . . . good." Hans had expected more of a fight and was just a bit disappointed that he didn't get one. "Then let's get set up to shoot that scene in sections."

"So," GAGE SAID, when they'd finished for the day. "How're you holding up?"

Tara smiled at him, snuggling into his side as he draped an arm around her neck. "I think my cheeks are permanently red from all the indelicate remarks, but I'll probably survive the scandal."

"After dinner do you want to go watch the dailies with Hans? Word is, you're pretty terrific in them."

Tara shook her head. "It's bad enough watching myself in the finished movie," she said. "I don't go through the agony of watching the dailies if I don't have to."

"How about a hand or two of poker, then? Pierce is hosting the game tonight."

"I'm a lousy player. I can never remember what beats what."

"Carly from Makeup and a couple of the grips are going to skip dinner and go into town to do some honky-tonkin'. We could tag along, if you'd like."

"No, thanks, I'm not up to a late night like that. Got close-ups tomorrow."

"Well, then, let's see, there's—"

Tara tilted her head to look up at him. "Are you by any chance trying to avoid being alone with me, Mr. Kingston?"

"Hell, no, Ms. Channing. I'm just trying to show you how polite and friendly I can be."

"Really," she drawled, both amused and touched by his effort to show her the friendship side of their relationship. "And are dailies and poker and honky-tonkin' your idea of friendly?"

"Unless you'd like to lock yourself in your trailer with me and make love until we can't see straight?"

Tara gave him one of her slanted, sideways glances. "I thought you'd never ask."

THE NEXT DAY'S PRODUCTION hit one snag after another. Not due to any sudden disappearances on the part of the female lead and the cinematographer but because the second male lead couldn't seem to "get into" his character.

They were supposed to be filming the big confrontation scene between Yuri and Yelena—the one where the budding young communist warns his sister "for the last time" to stay out of Party business and away from "that foreign instigator" who, of course, was Pierce's character. Jeremy Dean was having trouble relating to just how threatening he was supposed to be toward his fictional sister.

"Just exactly how menacing?" he demanded of Hans after flubbing the seventh take. "Do I mean it when I threaten to kill her if she doesn't obey me? Am I trying to scare her in order to protect her? What?" He threw his hands up and got right in the director's face. "I need some *direction* here."

"Twenty minute break, people," the assistant director shouted, not even waiting for Hans to confirm it. Everybody recognized that look in the director's eyes.

"He should take a page from that great immortal of Hollywood's Golden Age and just do it." Gage said a few minutes later as he dropped into a canvas chair beside Tara.

"Who's that?" she asked absently, her eyes still on the book in her lap. "That basketball player who does those commercials for Nike?"

"No, not Michael Jordan," Gage said, grinning at her bent head. "Spencer Tracy."

Tara looked up, feigned astonishment in her eyes. "Spencer Tracy played basketball?"

"No, Spencer Tracy didn't play basketball. Not as far as I know, anyway. Although," he mused, "I suppose it's possible he might have played a few hoops on the ol' MGM back lot with Clark Gable between takes. I'd like to have seen that."

"And Spencer Tracy said 'Just do it'?"

"Well, I'm paraphrasing, of course. But it was something like that. Someone once asked him to explain his acting method and he's supposed to have said he just made sure to hit his mark and remember his lines. Or words to that effect."

"Words for every actor to live by," Tara said, turning back to her book. "I'm sure Jeremy would appreciate hearing them."

Gage, predictably, failed to take the hint. "What's that you're reading?"

"Same thing I've been reading all week. *The Seven Pillars of Wisdom* by T. E. Lawrence."

"Kind of heavy going, isn't it?"

"Very."

"I remember reading it back in film school," Gage said. "The teacher had this crazy idea that it would give us more insight into the movie. I had to look up practically every other word in the dictionary to understand what the hell ol' T.E. was trying to say."

Tara looked up at that. "Really?" she asked in a pleased voice.

"Don't you?"

"Well, yes," she admitted, "but I didn't realize anybody else did."

"You didn't?" he said idly, just to keep her talking. He liked this "being friends" with her, he realized. It was a nice adjunct to the "being lovers" part of their relationship. "Why not?"

Tara sighed and closed her book. "I dropped out of high school in my junior year," she said as if she were confessing to mass murder. "There were a lot of family problems at the time and well . . ." She shrugged and looked down at the leather-bound book in her lap.

"I didn't realize T. E. Lawrence was on the reading list to get your G.E.D.," Gage said, understanding immediately what she was trying to say and curious about what she didn't say. *What kind of family problems?*

"Oh, he isn't," Tara informed him. "I got my G.E.D. in night school, right after I came to California. The teacher handed out a recommended reading list at the end of the class. Said a well-read person was a well-educated one. I'm about halfway through her list."

"I hope most of the books on it are more interesting than that one."

"Oh." Tara smiled and stroked a hand over the cover of the heavy book. "It's not that bad. Old T.E. was arrogant and pretentious but he led an interesting life."

"If you can wade through all the rhetoric." He leaned forward then and covered her hand on the book. "What kind of family problems made you drop out of school?" he asked.

"Oh, just the, ah . . . usual, you know."

"No, I don't know. Tell—"

"Places," yelled the A.D. "Places everybody. Break's over."

HE TRIED TO FIND OUT more later that night but she distracted him. First with her fevered body—the greatest diversionary tactic of all, as far as he was concerned— and then with outright evasions.

"I'd really rather not talk about it," she stressed. "It's depressing and boring and it was over a long time ago."

"Did your father abuse you?" he asked, thinking that that would go a long way in explaining the strange dichotomy he sensed in her. Women who had been sexually abused as children, he understood, often experienced conflict about their sexuality and tended to send out contradictory and confusing signals.

"I never knew my father," Tara told him. "He and my mother separated before I was born."

"Did you have a stepfather?"

"No. My mother never remarried." Nor, for the record, had she ever been married. But that was something Tara hadn't shared with anyone—ever. She rolled over in Gage's embrace and propped herself up on his chest. "Tell me how you got this scar," she ordered, touching her fingertip to the fine line of raised white tissue slicing through his left eyebrow in an effort to distract from a subject she didn't want to talk about. "And this one." She touched the dent on the bridge of his nose.

"Do you want the story I usually tell to make me look dashing to all the women?" He gathered her fingers in his and brought them to his mouth for a kiss. "Or do you want the truth?"

"You don't need to be any more dashing than you are," she said sternly. "The truth."

"Pierce hit me with a toy truck. A big, red, metal dump truck. He was four and I was almost six. I had to have three stitches in this one." He touched the scar on his eyebrow. "And I screamed bloody murder through the whole thing."

"Maybe you'd better tell me the dashing story, after all," Tara, deadpanned, and then wriggled away, giggling like a schoolgirl when he tried to tickle her.

"Quiet on the set," the A.D. hollered.

"Roll film," Hans said. "And...action."

With the perverse logic of the movie industry, they were finally getting around to filming the very first meeting between the Russian girl, Yelena Zdravkovich, and Nicolai Charnoff, who was posing as a government inspector from the newly formed Commonwealth of Independent States. In reality, the character was an American CIA agent attached to the new Kremlin to help stop the resurgence of old-style communism and turn the tide of popular opinion toward democracy.

It was a scene of great delicacy—short and seemingly inconsequential but vitally important for setting the tone between their two characters. It had to be played with just the right touch; blatant enough to foreshadow the relationship to come, subtle enough not to give everything away. They rehearsed it half-a-dozen times, with half-a-dozen different inflections on each word, until Hans was finally satisfied that his actors would give him what he wanted.

"My sister, Yelena," Jeremy said casually. "Yelena, this is Nicolai Charnoff. From Moscow," he added in subtle warning.

Tara ducked her head. "You are a long way from home." She gave Pierce a shy, assessing glance from under her lashes. In that one brief look, the theatergoer would read interest, speculation and instant sexual awareness—and would know, somehow, that men like Nicolai Charnoff were rare in Yelena's dreary little town.

"Yes," Pierce agreed, giving her his own assessing glance. There was speculation in his look, too. And not just sexual. With just the slightest narrowing of his eyes, Pierce conveyed the impression that he was sizing her up for her possible usefulness to his mission. "Very far."

"Give me a tight two-shot," Hans whispered to Gage, as Pierce and Tara stood there, covertly eyeing each other.

"It must be very lonely for you," Yelena said, and everyone who heard her was left with the distinct impression that she was lonely, too. Desperately, unbearably lonely. "To be so far away from your wife and family."

"I have no wife," Nicolai said, smiling at her.

"Yelena, come along now," snapped Yuri. "We will be late if you do not hurry."

She obeyed her brother instantly, leaving Nicolai standing alone on the wooden sidewalk in front of the bakery. And then, just when you thought she was completely cowed, she turned her head ever so slightly, giving him a sweet, secret smile and slanting, sideways a glance of invitation.

"Cut and print."

"YOU DON'T REALLY like acting much, do you?" Gage asked as they lay together in Tara's bed after a bout of tempestuous and tender loving.

"Why do you say that?"

"No specific reason." She felt his shoulder move under her head as he shrugged. "Just an impression I get from watching you do it. Not that you're not good at it," he hastened to assure her. "You're terrific—which you'd see if you'd watch the dailies—but you don't get the same...I don't know—the same *charge* out of it that Pierce does. Or Jeremy. It doesn't consume you the way it does them."

"No, I guess not," Tara agreed sleepily. "But I don't not like doing it. It's a good job. A lot better than waitressing." She yawned and burrowed into his shoulder. "The hours are long, though, and some of the side benefits leave something to be desired," she said dryly, referring to all the negative publicity that usually surrounded her, "but the pay is pretty terrific, especially for someone without much formal education. I've built myself up a nice little nest egg with what I've earned being Jessica. All very tidily invested in diversified mutual funds and real estate. My salary from this is going to go in the same place."

Gage chuckled and settled her more securely in his embrace.

"What?" she asked.

"You sound like Claire."

"Your sister?"

"Mmm-hmm. A hardheaded businesswoman if there ever was one. She didn't think much of acting, either. Quit, cold turkey, after almost eighteen years as one of the biggest child stars in Hollywood."

"Just like that?"

"Just like that," Gage affirmed. "Now she's one of the sharpest producers in the business."

"Must be nice," Tara said, snuggling deeper into the warmth of his arms.

"What's that?"

"Being able to chuck acting, just like that, and do something real with your life."

"Is that what you'd like to do?"

"That's what I'm *going* to do. As soon as my nest egg is big enough, I'm going to quit acting and live like a normal person."

"And do what?" Gage asked, intrigued.

"Go to college, maybe. Or get married and have a big family. Or both," she said serenely, smiling happily at the thought.

"AND WHAT HAVE WE HERE?" Pierce said a few days later in their trailer as he opened the latest express package from Claire. He pulled out a stack of newspapers. "Uh-oh," he said as a headline caught his eye. "Looks like you two are front-page news." He unfolded it and snapped it open. "Good God," he exclaimed. "I'm front-page news, too."

"What?" demanded Gage. "Let me see that." He snatched the paper out of his brother's hands as Tara picked up another one from the pile. "Tara Channing Pits Brother Against Brother," Gage read. "Newest Kingston Production In Jeopardy Over Tara's Sexploits."

Below the headlines were several recent pictures taken on the set. Tara and Pierce in a clinch from the movie; Tara and Gage relaxing in a pair of directors' chairs, looking intimate and cozy; Tara in Gage's arms as he carried her from the set after her fall, with Pierce hovering just behind them, looking worried. The text that went with the pictures was just as incriminating, truth and innuendo were twisted just enough to defy rebuttal.

Sexy Tara Channing is at it again. This time the renowned "Other Woman" has got herself involved in a cozy little ménage à trois in the wilds of Montana. Sources say she and superhunk, Pierce Kingston, are "just friends." But haven't we all heard that before? Big brother Gage is said to be her real love interest. For now.

"Where in *hell* do they get this stuff?" Gage exploded, throwing the paper down without bothering to turn to page six for the rest of the story.

"Now don't get all riled up," Pierce cautioned. "We knew this was going to happen sooner or later."

"That's not the worst of it," Tara said, stricken. Silently she handed Gage the paper she'd been scanning.

Kingston Brothers Feud Over Tara, it said. Under the two-inch headline was a doctored photograph of Gage and Pierce, appearing to glare at each other over the nude picture of Tara that had been spliced between them. Narrow black bars obscured the tips of her breasts and the triangle of hair at the tops of her thighs, making her look a lot more provocative than she would have if they'd left the picture alone. There was also a publicity still of Alyssa, tucked into a corner on the front page, with the caption My Husband's Secret Obsession With Tara Channing Broke Up My Marriage.

"Damn it!" Gage cursed.

"At least they spelled everybody's name right," Pierce commented, trying to lighten the mood. "And it's only a seven-day wonder, anyway. Next week Demi Moore or Delta Burke will do something to push you right off the front page and people will forget all about this."

Gage crumpled up the paper and threw it down in disgust. It landed on the floor at Tara's feet.

"Gage?" she said hesitantly, her voice quavering a bit. She could see him retreating right before her eyes, backing away, although he hadn't actually moved an inch. "Gage?" she said again, and held out her hand.

"I can't deal with this right now," he said, ignoring her proffered hand. "I'm sorry. I know this is different from the last time. I know you're not anything like Alyssa. That you didn't have anything to do with this filth but—" he grabbed his sheepskin jacket off a chair "—I just can't deal with it right now."

He slammed out of the trailer, leaving Tara and Pierce staring at each other in dumbfounded silence.

"They raked him over the coals pretty good during his divorce," Pierce said after a moment, trying to explain his brother's reaction to the woman who sat staring at him with the eyes of a wounded doe. "Alyssa fed 'em a lot of garbage. A lot of half-truths and innuendo and outright lies that were close enough to the facts to be believed, even by people who should have known better."

"I know," Tara whispered. "Believe me, I know."

"It wasn't just the tabloids, either. It made *People*. It's a hard thing for a man to admit his wife was just using him to advance her career," he added when she didn't respond. "It's even harder when he has to wear horns in public. It's the kind of thing that leaves a lot of scars. And it tends to make a man, well, suspicious. Especially a man like Gage."

"Especially when it appears to be happening again," Tara said.

"Oh, no, he knows you're not responsible. It's just that he's feeling kind of vulnerable and exposed right now. And he's not thinking straight. Give him a little while to think about it and he'll be back. You'll see, in a little while he'll be apologizing all over you for acting like such an ass."

"Maybe." She stood and reached for her down parka. *But I don't think so.*

"Why don't you stay here until he gets back?" Pierce suggested, wanting to comfort her but not knowing exactly how. "I'll make you some tomato soup and a grilled-cheese sandwich," he offered. "And some hot chocolate." It was what his mother had always fixed for him and his brother and sister when they were feeling bad about something. "How does that sound?"

"I'm really not very hungry."

"We could watch a video. I've got Abbott and Costello. They're always good for a laugh."

"No. Thank you, Pierce. I know you're trying to help but I need to be alone for a while." She slipped into her parka and zipped it up. "I'll see you tomorrow morning," she said, digging through the pockets for her gloves and muffler to avoid having to look at him. She didn't want him to see the tears clouding her eyes. "Bright and early, okay?"

"Yeah, sure. Okay."

She stepped out into the cold night air, shivering despite the heavy jacket and gloves and the purple muffler around her neck.

"You knew it was going to end," she told herself, squaring her shoulders against the pain. "You just didn't think it would happen so soon."

10

THE NEXT MORNING Gage still hadn't returned.

Hans threw a fit, of course, but then he settled down when it was pointed out that Gage had already laid all the groundwork, cinematographically speaking, for the look of the film, and that the second cameraman was as talented and capable as anyone in the industry as far as actual camera operation was concerned. The movie wouldn't suffer, whether Gage was there or not. And, in all likelihood, he'd be back before long, anyway. A day or two wasn't going to make any difference to anyone, not even to the ever-present tyranny of the budget. Hans grumbled about irresponsibility and unprofessional conduct but he adjusted to the situation.

He didn't adjust quite so easily to the media circus that followed. Reporters from all the major tabloids arrived on the second day of Gage's absence, having heard from God-only-knew-where about the latest development in the Kingston-Channing affair, as they'd started calling it. Desperate for the tiniest tidbit of gossip, they interviewed any of the locals they could find who were willing to talk about whatever they may have seen on the days they were employed as extras. They hollered questions at grips and technicians and actors whenever they could get close enough to the filming. And they dug up every old scandal and story—and there were a lot of them—involving Tara or any one of the Kingstons, rehashing them in print alongside "new" stories about rivalry and disruption on the set.

Tara lived in a constant state of dread that the reporters would finally dig up the past she had never told anyone about. But each day, when she opened the papers to read the morning's headlines, there was never any mention of Bobby Clay Bishop and the part he had played in her life all those years ago. She could only be grateful.

Neither Hans's theatrics nor Pierce's deliberately more good-natured and measured arguments for sanity nor even Claire Kingston's soft-voiced threats of legal action, when she arrived two days later, could convince the reporters they'd find a better story elsewhere.

The biting cold, the lack of comfortable accommodations and the extra security that Claire brought with her to chase the reporters away from the location site when they ventured too close might have deterred some of them if the story had been exclusively about Tara or just one of the Kingstons. But a scandal involving Hollywood's most notorious other woman and *both* Kingston brothers . . . ah, now there was a story worth frostbite and a few lawsuits.

Tara liked Claire Kingston immediately. She had the same rich sable hair as one brother and the same brilliant blue eyes as the other. Her ivory skin and quiet elegance were innate and effortless. Her ballerina grace was the kind that came from years of practice at the barre. And her calm, no-nonsense business mien was a result, Tara was sure, of years of holding her own with the more flamboyant members of the Kingston clan.

"I've had my assistant check with all the police departments, ambulance services and hospitals within a tristate area to rule out the possibility of an accident or foul play," she informed them, setting her briefcase down on the floor beside the coffee table in her brothers' trailer. She perched on the edge of the sofa and, with a precise little flick of her wrist, smoothed her trim gray skirt over enviably trim thighs. "Which leads us to the conclusion that he left voluntarily."

"Which I told you on the phone," Pierce said.

Claire ignored him as if he hadn't spoken. "So—" she looked at Tara, her brilliant blue eyes shrewd and searching "—did he say or do anything—anything at all—that might give you an idea as to where he was going or how long he intended to be gone?" she asked, as if Tara was the one in the best position to know.

"No. He just said he couldn't deal with it. Or—" Tara's voice quavered but she controlled it "—or me. And then he left. I thought he'd be gone a couple of hours, at most. Maybe all night if he went into town. In fact, until the next morning I thought that's what had happened and that he'd just gone to his own trailer when he came back instead of, uh—" she colored slightly, as if the entire world didn't already know she was sleeping with Claire Kingston's brother "—coming to mine." She lifted her hands, palms up. "I'm sorry. I wish I could be more help."

"It's not your fault," Claire said kindly, reaching over to pat Tara's knee. "The fault for this whole mess belongs squarely on the shoulders of my knot-headed big brother."

"Oh, no, I—" Tara began, attempting to shield Gage from blame.

"He came on to you like gangbusters, didn't he?" Claire eyed her speculatively. "He took one look, decided you were what he wanted and wouldn't take no for an answer." Her glance at her brother was heavy with significance. "Isn't that right?"

"Well, yes, in a way but—" Tara began.

"He went after her like a bulldog after a meaty bone," Pierce said.

"And then he has the unmitigated gall to be surprised when it ends up in the tabloids." Claire shook her head.

"If it's really important that we locate him," Pierce said carefully, "I'd suggest you send someone up to the cabin at Mammoth." No one outside the immediate family knew the cabin in Mammoth, California, existed. "If he wanted to make absolutely sure of avoiding the press, that's where he'd go."

"I agree," Claire said. "But unless anyone here needs him for a specific reason . . ." She raised one perfectly arched brow at Tara.

Tara blushed faintly, wondering if they knew . . . No, it was impossible because she'd only just begun to suspect it herself. She shook her head.

"Are you sure?" Claire asked.

"I'm sure," Tara said firmly, deciding it was her own dawning suspicions that made her read into Claire's innocent questions something that wasn't there.

"Well, okay, if you're sure," Claire said doubtfully, "then I suggest we leave him to his own devices. If he's as smart as I think he is, he'll be back before long."

"I'll go get him for you if you really want him," Pierce offered to Tara. "Hog-tie him if I have to."

Tara smiled her first real smile in four days. "Thanks but no thanks."

"Smart girl," Claire agreed. "If he has to be hog-tied, who wants him? Right?"

"Ah . . . right," Tara said.

"We're agreed then?" Claire looked at her brother for confirmation.

"Agreed," Pierce said.

And Tara had the strangest feeling that a whole other conversation had just taken place, right alongside the one she'd been involved in.

"Well." Claire picked up her briefcase and stood. "Business awaits and I have a plane to catch," she said briskly. "Tara—" she bent down and kissed her on the cheek, leaving Tara blinking in astonishment "—it's been a real pleasure meeting you," she said warmly. "I look forward to getting to know you better when you're back in Los Angeles. Pierce," she said, tucking her free hand into the crook of his arm. "Walk me to the car, please."

TWO NIGHTS LATER, sitting on the edge of her bed with her hairbrush in her hand, Tara accepted the inevitable. Her period was late. And in all her life, since the day she became a woman, her period had been late only once before. That time, she'd been seventeen years old and pregnant with Bobby Clay Bishop's baby. This time, she was twenty-five and the father was Gage Kingston.

Other than that, she thought, the two situations really weren't much different.

She was still on her own. Still a woman alone, facing the consequences of her folly. An unwed mother—again.

"Only this time," she vowed, putting the hairbrush down to spread both hands protectively over her lower abdomen. "I'll take care of myself. And you," she said to the tiny life inside her. "I'll go to the doctor and I'll rest and I'll eat all the right foods. And I won't let anyone make me feel ashamed for letting you happen." She patted her stomach gently, soothingly. "I won't let anything hurt you," she promised. "And you'll be born healthy and whole and happy."

Getting up from the bed, she moved across her small bedroom and pulled open the drawer that held her nightgowns. Thrusting her hand under a pile of white cambric and pastel ribbons, she pulled out a tiny pink sweater. Taking it back to the bed with her, she lay down on the satin sheets and cuddled it to her cheek. There was a soft smile on her face as she drifted off to sleep.

TARA AWOKE in the middle of the night, roused from an uneasy sleep by the soft creak of the trailer door opening. She lay perfectly still in the big bed for a moment, her eyes staring into the darkness, her ears straining for another sound, wondering if one of the reporters had found his or her way past the guards.

They'd caught one of them in Pierce's trailer just after the lunch break that same afternoon, rummaging through the pile of papers on the coffee table. It'd been a victory, of sorts, because, caught in the act as he'd been, they'd been able to have him arrested and carted away. And he hadn't found anything to give him any insights into the "situation" because there wasn't anything to find.

"But what do you want to bet that by tomorrow night everybody in L.A. will know I'm considering *The Devil's Game* for my next picture?" Pierce said, referring to the script that his sister had sent and which had been left lying open on the coffee table. "Claire's going to want my head if that drives the price up."

Tara's ears pricked up at the sound of soft footfalls. They became more distinct as whoever it was crossed the bare floor of the kitchenette toward the bedroom at the back of the trailer.

Tara debated screaming bloody murder and then, in the next second, decided that doing so would only scare her midnight visitor away. Better, she thought vindictively, to get a good look at whoever it was and *then* scream for help so she could have the intruder arrested for trespassing and unlawful entry. Maybe even mental distress. She was, after all, an actress. She should be able to convince a jury that having a reporter break into her trailer in the middle of the night had resulted in severe psychological upset. Everybody knew actors were unstable to begin with.

She put her hand on the blankets, intending to flip them back, and met the intruder on her feet when a broad-shouldered shadow filled the doorway. She froze in midmotion. Not a reporter, after all.

Gage had come back.

She let her hand fall to the bed and waited. Did he intend to just slip into bed beside her as if nothing had happened? Would he expect to make love to her like before, as if nothing had changed? And would she let him if he did?

He tiptoed into the room and eased himself down onto the edge of the bed. "Tara?" he whispered. His hand hovered over her for a moment, as if he would touch her, and then he pulled it back. "Tara, wake up."

"I'm awake," she said into the darkness.

They were silent for a second or two, neither of them knowing what to say or how to say it because so much depended on what the other said first.

"Where—" Tara began.

"Tara, I—" Gage said at the same time, his voice cutting across hers. There was another second of uncomfortable silence and then, "Ladies first," Gage said.

"Where were you?" she asked, trying not to sound accusing or demanding. "Where did you go?"

"I ended up in a place called Wolf Creek."

"Wolf Creek? Do you know someone there?"

"No. That's just where I was when I skidded off the road."

She gasped and sat up with a start. "Are you all right? Were you hurt?" she asked, reaching out to snap on the bedside light so she could see for herself. "You *were* hurt!" she cried, lifting her hand to touch the mottled purple bruise on his cheek.

He took her hand in his, pulling it away from his face. "I'm fine," he assured her, pressing her fingers to the bed to keep from taking her into his arms. "It's just a little bruise from where I hit the steering wheel. Nothing serious."

"You should have called," she said. "Everyone was worried about you. Your sister had people checking the hospitals."

"I know. I'm sorry. I *should* have called. I would have if it'd been anything serious. But it wasn't."

"Tell me what happened."

"I hit a patch of ice and skidded off the road and into a fence post. A trucker came by maybe twenty minutes later and gave me a ride into town to find a garage with a tow truck. After that, I ended up hanging around in a motel while they replaced a busted radiator. I would have been back sooner if it hadn't been for that."

"You should have called," she repeated. "Someone would have come for you."

"I didn't want someone to come for me. I needed time to think this whole thing through." He let go of her hand and ran his fingers through his hair. "To come to a few conclusions before I came back."

"And have you?" Tara asked, dreading the answer she could already see in his eyes.

"Yes, I have."

She waited, knowing that what he had to say was going to break her heart. She squared her shoulders under the fabric of her fine lawn nightgown, determined not to let it show.

"I can't go through it again," he said quietly, looking down at the white satin bedspread as he spoke. "I've thought about it, examined it from every angle, and I just can't go through it again. Having my private life dissected for public consumption, every little thing gist for the national gossip mill, putting up with all the speculation and innuendo about your latest love affair every time you even smile at another man. Call it pride or male vanity, but I just can't do it. I can't be the man in the 'other woman's' life. It might be different if we were in love, but we aren't." He paused expectantly, as if waiting for her to comment.

"No, we aren't," she agreed as her heart broke clean in two.

"If we were in love, then we might be able to deal with all the hassle and headaches involved. But we're not."

"No," Tara echoed, unconsciously slipping her hand under the blankets to cover her stomach. "We're not."

He took a deep breath. "So, I think the best thing to do is end it here and now." He risked a glance at her to see how she was taking it. She met his eyes calmly, even serenely, with all the innate dignity of a true lady. "A clean break." He smiled ruefully. "The way you said we should have done in the beginning."

"A clean break," she parroted. "Yes, I think that's probably best."

"God, I'm sorry for all this, Tara. Not for what we've shared—I'll never regret that—but for the last few days. You don't deserve all this ugly speculation. All the nastiness. And you certainly didn't deserve to have me run out on you and let you face it on your own."

"I wasn't alone," she said, automatically trying to reassure him. "Pierce was here." *And the baby.* "And Claire called in the troops. It will all blow over in a week or two, anyway," she added, sounding as if that were her only concern. "A new victim will do something outrageous and the tabloids will be howling after a new scandal."

"Then you don't want my head on a platter?"

"Of course not. Don't be silly. I knew the risks I was taking, the same as you." *Better than you.*

"Are we still friends?" He laid his hand out, palm up, on the bedspread.

She took her hand out from under the covers. "Friends," she said and put it into his without a moment's hesitation.

He squeezed her fingers tight. *There should be something else to say,* he thought. *Some clever last words to make this easier.* He couldn't think of anything. He lifted her hand to his lips and pressed a quick kiss to the back of it in lieu of the goodbye that was inexplicably caught in his throat. "I'm sorry it turned out this way," he managed, and stood to leave.

A small scrap of fabric fell to the floor as he rose, brushed off the bed by his movement. He bent down to pick it up. It was tiny and pink, expertly fashioned out of fine baby-soft wool and unmistakably sized for a newborn.

"Tara?" He looked, suddenly, as if he'd been hit between the eyes with a two-by-four. "Are you *pregnant?*"

"No," she said quickly. *Too quickly?* "Of course not."

"Then what's this?"

"It's a memento." She made a grab at it and failed. "Give it to me, please."

"A memento of what?"

"I don't really think that's any of your business."

"Under the circumstances I think it is. You said you'd let me know if you were pregnant. You said you'd know in a week, at most." She could practically see him counting backward. "But we've made love every night for the last three weeks."

"Except for the last five nights," she pointed out, hoping he would believe her and go away.

"You had your period while I was gone?"

"Yes."

"That seems a bit convenient."

"Once in a while it happens that way." She held out her hand. "Give me the sweater back. Please." She tried not to sound as desperate as she felt. If he didn't go away soon she was going to break down and tell him the truth. And she knew he didn't want to hear that. No matter what he said, he didn't really want to hear it.

"You don't have to be afraid to tell me if you're pregnant," he said gently, feeling tenderness and something suspiciously like happiness well up inside him. If she was pregnant . . . "I said we'd work it out together and we will."

"There's nothing to work out."

"Then what's this?"

Tara took a deep breath and told him part of the truth because she knew it was the only thing he would believe. "When I was seventeen I got pregnant," she said in a flat, carefully unemotional voice that only emphasized the pain. "There were complications and the baby came three months early. She lived for five days in an incubator. That sweater is the only thing I have left of her."

"That's why you dropped out of school."

"Yes." She held out her hand again. "May I have it now, please?"

He gave it to her. "Why are you sleeping with it now? Tonight?" he said, still suspicious. Still, in some strange way, hoping. "Why haven't I seen it before?"

"Because sometimes I miss her more than others."

"But why tonight in particular?"

"Because when my period was late, I started fantasizing about having another baby and missing the one that died," she said, honestly. "When I realized I wasn't pregnant after all, it made me a little sad."

"You *wanted* to be pregnant?" Why did the thought give him such a thrill?

"No, not really." She stroked the sweater lightly with her fingertips to avoid looking at him. Lying was always easier if you didn't have to look your victim in the eye. "It was just a female sort of wishful thinking, brought on by sentiment and hormones."

"I don't know what to say."

"Don't say anything," she advised. "Just go." She looked up at him from under her lashes, quickly, and then down at the sweater again. "I have to do my big death scene tomorrow," she reminded him, wishing he'd leave before she fell completely to pieces, "and I need to get some sleep."

"Will you be all right?"

"I'll be fine. I *am* fine."

He hesitated for a moment longer, looking as if he wanted to say something more.

"A clean break, remember?" Tara said.

Without another word, he turned and left.

Tara waited until she heard the trailer door close and then she picked up the tiny sweater and draped it over her stomach. "Sleep tight, little baby," she whispered, smoothing the material over her belly.

THEY SHOT Tara's final scene the next morning with a minimum of rehearsal because Hans thought it was the kind of scene that benefited from the spontaneous expression of emotion. He didn't want to wring the "juice" out of it with too many run-throughs.

"I want courage and deathless love," he said to Tara as she sat in the makeup chair having her glowing complexion paled to a suitable deathlike pallor. Fake blood was then liberally applied to the front of her blouse and down one arm.

Yelena had been shot in the chest by Feodor Bartlinsky, the machine-shop foreman who had ensnared her brother in his dreams of glory. Now she was about to die in her lover's arms.

"I want pain and rage," Hans said to Pierce as the actor positioned himself behind the prop door. "At her brother and Feodor Bartlinsky. At fate. At yourself for getting her into this situation."

"Places everybody," called the A.D.

Tara lowered herself to the floor and lay facedown, flinging one arm out as if she had fallen in a heap. Someone from Makeup crouched down and spread her hair out around her head. Someone else arranged her shawl by her side as if she had dropped it before she'd fallen.

"Roll film," Hans ordered. "And . . . action."

Pierce burst through the door of the small house, panting as if he'd been running. "Yelena! Oh, my God. Yelena." He knelt down beside her and felt for her pulse. Mouthing a prayer of thanks at finding her alive, he slipped an arm under her shoulders and carefully, tenderly turned her onto her back. The blood-soaked front of her blouse came into view. The camera lingered there for a moment and then panned upward, focusing on the horror in Pierce's face. "Yelena," he whispered, anguish and rage warring for supremacy in his voice. The awful knowledge of her imminent death was in his eyes.

The camera did an extreme close-up of Tara's face as her eyelids fluttered and then opened. "Nicolai?"

"Yes, darling, it's Nicolai."

"I'm cold," she said piteously, like a frightened child.

He picked the shawl up off the floor and covered her with it, tenderly tucking it around her as he turned her into his embrace. "There, now, my love. Is that better?"

"Promise," she said, making the word less than a whisper of sound.

"Hush, don't try to talk. Save your strength." He began to rock her slowly, back and forth, murmuring senseless words of love and comfort to ease her dying.

Courage and deathless love, Tara reminded herself. She thought about the end of her relationship with Gage and about the baby he didn't know she carried. Something in her face softened and became stronger all at once. "Remember your promise," she said, struggling to form the words.

"Anything, darling. Anything." He pressed a fervent kiss on her forehead, and then on her cheek. "Tell me."

"Yuri," she said. "Save him."

Again the camera zoomed in for an extreme close-up, focusing on Nicolai's hands as they clenched Yelena's shawl. "Yes," he promised in a strangled voice. "I'll save him. For you, my love."

She lifted her hand then, slowly, obviously trying to touch her lover's face. Nicolai grasped it in his, oblivious to the blood that smeared it, and brought it to his lips. He pressed a deep kiss into her palm.

Yelena smiled. "My love," she said, and everyone there heard the love and longing in her voice, the regret for what would never be. She ran her fingertip over the bow of his lip, and then her hand dropped and her head fell back and her body went limp as death claimed her.

Nicolai gave a fierce cry of pain and rage. Gathering her close, he buried his face in the curve of her neck and began to sob. Gage's camera zoomed in on the strong, blood-smeared fist clutched in her hair, then on the broad shoulders shuddering in grief and, finally, on the slim, bloodied hand lying, palm up, on the cold linoleum floor.

And then Nicolai stood, lifting his dead lover in his arms, to carry her to the narrow bed where they had made love. One camera shot him from the back—his wide strong torso and shoulders framed by Yelena's flowing skirt and the long fall of her hair dangling over his arm—as he moved across the room. Another camera shot him from the front to show his face as he lowered her onto the bed. He placed her hands at her sides and brushed back her hair, then pulled up a blanket, tucking it around her as if to keep her warm while she slept. When he strode toward the door there was fierce purpose in every step as tears tracked through the blood on his lean cheek.

There was a long moment of appreciative silence when the door slammed behind him. "Cut and print!" Hans hollered as the cast and crew broke into applause.

11

"YOU'VE GOT TO GET ME OUT of my soap opera contract, Margo," Tara said, pacing back and forth on the plush lavender-colored carpet in front of her agent's desk. "I don't care how you do it. Just do it."

"Wouldn't you rather go on a hiatus? They could put Jessica in a coma or something. Maybe send her off on a world tour for a few months. And then, when you've got your priorities straight again, they can bring her back."

"My priorities are straight," Tara said. "Believe me, they are. And I want out of my contract. Tell them it's an act of God." She stopped pacing for a moment to confront Margo directly. "I do have an act-of-God clause, don't I?"

"You do," Margo said. "Although it would be helpful to know just what act of the Almighty I'm being called on to use during negotiations with the studio."

"I'm pregnant."

For just a moment, some of Margo Melrose's legendary cool deserted her. "Pregnant?" she echoed stupidly.

"Yes, pregnant. As in with child. As in an interesting condition. As in knocked up. Pregnant."

"At least some of the rumors about you and the Kingston brothers are true, then." She raised a silky black eyebrow. "Which one is the father?"

"Gage," Tara admitted. "Pierce and I are just friends."

"Are congratulations in order? Or should I offer my condolences?"

Tara smiled. "Oh, congratulations." She put her hand on her still-flat stomach. "Definitely congratulations."

"Well, this is a surprise, I must say. Are you planning a wedding or is this going to be one of those unwise modern relationships where no vows are exchanged?"

"It isn't going to be any kind of relationship at all except between me and the baby."

Margo frowned. "*Most* unwise."

"Not in this case," Tara said.

"Do you want to tell me about it?"

Tara hesitated for a moment. She was an intensely private person, one who tended to keep her real feelings hidden even from those she trusted most and had known the longest. But Margo was her friend, as well as her agent, and she needed to tell someone. Besides, she was going to need Margo's help and it wasn't fair to ask for it without telling her the reason why.

"Yes," Tara said finally, and sat down in the chair in front of Margo's desk. "Yes, I think I do want to tell you about it."

It took her a moment to marshal her thoughts, to decide just where to begin so that Margo would understand what had happened and why she had chosen the course she had. Margo sat quietly and waited.

"I fell in love," Tara said at last, as if that explained everything. Which it did. "Almost from the first moment I looked into his eyes. I tried to fight it because I could tell that it wasn't the same for him, that he was only looking at me the way so many other men have looked at me. But he was persistent—" she smiled, remembering "—and forceful and charming and I wanted him so much. So very, very much," she said softly. "And so I said yes."

"And ended up pregnant." Margo shook her head. "Didn't he do anything to protect you? Didn't you *insist* on protection?"

"It wasn't his fault," Tara said, defending him. "He brought something to use but we forgot that first night. He insisted that I tell him when I knew whether or not I was pregnant. He said we would deal with it together but—"

"Then why isn't he with you now?"

"Because I didn't tell him."

"Why not?"

"Because it had all started to fall apart by then. Because he'd already said that he couldn't be the man in the 'other woman's' life." She spread her hands. "What good would it have done to tell him if he feels like that?"

"Because no matter what he thinks he can or can't do, he should be with you. Helping you through this. Taking responsibility for his actions."

"No." The word rang with irrevocable finality. "My mother ruined her life trying to make my father live up to his responsibilities to us. And then she nearly ruined mine by trying to make Bobby Clay Bishop live up to his responsibilities to me."

There was a moment of silence as Margo absorbed that. "You had a baby before," she said slowly.

"When I was seventeen."

"And they made you have an abortion or give it up for adoption," Margo guessed. "And that's why you want this baby so much."

"No," Tara said. "That baby died five days after she was born." She covered her stomach protectively with both hands. "And that's why I want *this* baby so much. That, and because it's Gage's baby."

"You should tell him."

"No," Tara said again.

"You know that as soon as the tabloids get wind of your pregnancy, he's going to find out, anyway. And what happened in Montana is going to look like a tea party in comparison to the feeding frenzy there'll be when they find out."

"They won't find out about it."

"How can you say that, Tara? You know what they're like. Sooner or later, they seem to find out about everything."

"Because you're going to help me make sure they don't."

"Me?"

"Yes, you." She leaned forward in her chair and put her hands on the edge of Margo's desk. "You're going to get me out of my contract without telling anyone the real reason, and then I'm going to disappear."

"Disappear?"

"From television. From the movies. From Hollywood."

"But your career, your life . . ."

"My career's not important. Nothing's important except my baby."

"It takes money to raise a baby, have you thought of that?"

"I have money. You know that, because you've been investing it for me. It's more money than most people ever dream of having and more than enough for the way I intend to live from now on."

"And how's that?"

"I'm going to sell my house in the hills and then—"

"But you're so proud of that house," Margo objected. "You were so pleased when you bought it."

"It's just a house." Tara shrugged. "I want you to sell it for me—I'll give you power of attorney—and then I want you to help me find something smaller in a safe, secure little suburb in some little town where no one would ever think to look for Tara Channing."

"And then what?"

"And then I'll move in and wait for my baby to be born."

"And your career? According to the buzz around town you're going to be hot when *The Promise* is released."

Tara snapped her fingers. "*That* for my career," she said. "It doesn't matter."

Margo sat back in her chair and looked hard at her client. "I can't talk you out of this?"

"No."

She sighed. "All right then," she said, pulling a lined yellow tablet toward her, "let's talk about where you think you might want to live."

"WHERE THE *HELL* IS SHE?" Gage exploded, pacing around his sister's elegant office like a caged wolf. "No one at her studio knows anything except that she's left the show permanently. Her house is on the market. Her agent isn't talking. Even the tabloids are playing guessing games. So what the hell is she up to?"

"I'd say it's fairly obvious," Claire said matter-of-factly. "She doesn't want to be found."

"Why the hell not?"

She arched her eyebrow at him. "I suspect you'd know the answer to that better than anyone," she said mildly.

"Well, damn it, I don't!"

"I don't know why you're making such a fuss about all this, anyway," commented Pierce from his seat on Claire's gray brocade love seat. He put his white china teacup and saucer down on the polished marquetry table in front of him and hooked a leg over one of its arms, slouching down into his usual loose-limbed position. "You were the one who said you wanted to put an end to the relationship in the first place, I'd think you'd be happy that she took you at your word."

"Well, I'm not," Gage growled.

"Yes, we can see that," Claire said dryly. She got up and came around the delicate Queen Anne table she used for a desk. Hitching the skirt of her trim linen suit up a bit, she perched on a corner. "I think we'd both be interested in knowing why not." She looked at her other brother and smiled. "Wouldn't we, Pierce?"

"Yes, indeedy," Pierce drawled.

Gage stopped his pacing to stare at his brother and sister. Until this very minute, he'd thought they were intelligent human beings with more than the average allocation of sensitivity, kindness and compassion. Now, he wasn't so sure.

Couldn't they see what was right before their eyes?

Tara was missing.

Gone!

And there was a great big, bleeding hole where his heart used to be.

Claire leaned forward on the edge of the desk. "Do you even *know* why you're acting like a crazed beast?" she asked softly. "Do you have any idea at all?"

"She's gone," he said bleakly.

"Just like you wanted," Pierce taunted.

"Damn it, she's gone!" Gage repeated. His hands clenched into fists at his sides. "And I don't know if I can live without her."

Pierce grinned. "Well, *now* we're getting someplace," he said to Claire.

GAGE PRESENTED HIMSELF at Margo Melrose's offices later that same afternoon, convinced that a face-to-face confrontation would get him the information he wanted. Talking to her on the telephone certainly hadn't done much good.

He was prepared to be charming, as only a born-and-bred Kingston could be, but her continued refusals to cooperate wore his patience thin in record time.

"Damn it," he roared, finally, bringing his fist down on her desk. "No one's seen hide nor hair of her for nearly a month. I want to know where she is."

Margo didn't even flinch. He was big and angry and a powerful force in Hollywood, but Margo Melrose would probably die before she'd let herself be intimidated by a mere man.

"I'm sorry, Mr. Kingston," she said calmly, with every bit of her legendary cool. "But Ms. Channing has given me strict instructions not to divulge her whereabouts to anyone. I would be committing a serious breach of client confidentiality if I were to tell you where she is."

"I'm not just anybody," Gage bit out, consciously using his status as a Kingston for the first time in his life. "Ms. Channing was working on a Kingston film and she hasn't fulfilled all the conditions of her contract."

"Really?" Margo raised an eyebrow. "And what conditions might those be?"

Gage ran a hand through his hair. "Looping," he said, referring to the process in which dialogue is rerecorded in a sound studio for more clarity. "Publicity."

"It was my understanding in speaking with your sister that the movie isn't anywhere near finished yet. You've got two weeks' worth of interior scenes still to shoot on the soundstage here in L.A., and then approximately six weeks of location work in…Moscow, isn't it?"

Gage nodded.

"In which case, Ms. Channing has a few months yet before she has to worry about being in breach of her contract with Kingston Productions." She straightened a pile of papers on her desk. "Perhaps if you'd like to give me a message for her," she suggested, "I could see that she gets it."

"You won't tell me where she is?"

"No, Mr. Kingston," she said firmly. "I won't."

THE NEXT DEVELOPMENT in the Channing-Kingston affair hit the checkout stands two days later. Tara Channing Pregnant With Kingston Baby, the headlines blared, But Which Kingston?

Quoting "reliable sources," the article went on to say that Tara Channing had been seen entering the offices of a prominent Los Angeles obstetrician and "further investigation" had revealed the information that she was indeed pregnant. What followed were several columns full of smarmy and titillating speculation as to which Kingston brother had fathered her "love child," and a discussion of possible reasons why neither one of the men in question was standing by her now.

One small consolation in the whole sorry mess was that, for the first time in her tabloid career, Tara Channing was being cast the innocent victim. For some reason the writer had chosen to portray her as a young woman whose life and career had been ruined after she'd been taken scurrilous advantage of and then tossed aside by the privileged and unprincipled scions of decadent movie royalty.

It made for heady reading.

Less heady, at least to Tara, were the mangled "facts" one tabloid reporter had finally managed to dig up about her past. They had the dates right and the place, but almost everything else was wrong. The kindly old doctor who had attended the birth declined to comment, citing doctor-patient confidentiality. Her mother, who still lived in Clayville, had flatly denied the story.

Which left Bobby Clay Bishop, the only other person who had known even part of what had happened, to give the story to the press. There was a picture of him—a prematurely balding man, grinning into the camera as if he had done something praiseworthy in failing to stand by the girl he'd gotten pregnant all those years ago.

"Pompous ass," Tara said, throwing the paper down in disgust. As it landed on the table in front of her, a startling thought formed itself in her mind.

With dawning awareness, she recognized that Bobby Clay had always been a pompous ass, even when he was seventeen and the best looking, most popular boy in Clayville High School.

She smiled to herself, realizing that, with that one thought, she was suddenly free of the past. She would always mourn the baby she had lost, of course, but all the rest was gone. The shame. The anger. The fear. It was all gone.

Two days later, Tara abruptly stopped watching "Entertainment Tonight" in the middle of the broadcast and called Margo.

"How do they find out all this stuff?" she wailed.

"Well, according to the report, someone saw you going into the doctor's office," Margo told her calmly. "Which is possible but not probable. Because, if that had been the case, that someone would more than likely

have followed you home and you'd have a pack of reporters on your doorstep right now."

"Oh, my God," Tara flicked back the curtain on her
window to check.

"Relax," Margo said. "I doubt they know where you
are."

"How can you be so sure?"

"Because I'll bet what really happened is that the re-
ceptionist or a nurse told one of her friends you'd been
in, and that friend told someone else who just happened to know someone who works for a tabloid."

"Can they do that?" Tara asked. "Is it legal? I thought
doctors had to guard a person's privacy."

"Whether it's legal or not is a moot point. They *have*
done it. So the next thing we have to worry about is
making sure they don't find out where you live."

"Oh, God, yes," Tara agreed fervently. She didn't
care about the negative publicity; in the scheme of
things it just wasn't important anymore. But she did
care about the possible inconvenience of a dozen reporters camped out on her doorstep. Her new neigh-
bors wouldn't like it at all. And Gage would find out
where she was. She wasn't ready for that.

"The first thing you're going to have to do is change
doctors, kiddo," Margo advised. "I'd suggest someone
who isn't known as the best obstetrician in Los Angeles," she said dryly.

"PREGNANT?" GAGE SAID when Claire handed him a
copy of the tabloid. "Pregnant! I asked her point blank
and she told me she was sure she wasn't."

"And maybe she isn't," Claire said soothingly. "That scandal sheet isn't the most reliable source of news, remember. The story could be a complete fabrication."

"But you don't think it is, do you?"

"Do you?" Claire countered.

"No." Gage crumpled the paper in his fist. "No, I think their reliable source got it right this time," he said, thinking of the events of that last night, thinking of the look on her face and the strange note in her voice. She'd lied to him. "Tara's pregnant all right."

"What are you going to do about it?"

"I'm going to put an end to this farce."

GAGE STORMED into Margo's office less than twenty minutes later, sweeping past the agitated secretary to fling open the door to the agent's inner sanctum.

"I'm sorry, Ms. Melrose," said the young woman who'd tried to block his path. "I couldn't stop him." She cast a fearful glance at Gage's furious face. "Do you want me to call the police?"

"No, there's no need to call the police," Margo said, giving Gage a stern look. "I'm sure Mr. Kingston will behave himself." She smiled at her secretary. "That will be all for now, Jennifer. Thank you."

The secretary backed out of the office reluctantly, obviously loathe to leave her employer with a madman.

Gage waited until the door was closed. "I want to know where she is," he said without preamble. "And I want to know right now."

"As I told you before, she's—"

"*Now,*" he said, his deadly calm a lot more intimidating than his rage had been.

Margo drew herself up to her full height, which at five feet in her heels, barely brought her head even with his chest. "I don't know what you think gives you the right to be mak—"

Gage threw the paper he was still clutching down on her desk. "This gives me the right," he said, indicating the headlines with a flick of his wrist. "She's pregnant with my child and I want to know where she is."

"So you can do what, Mr. Kingston? Just what exactly will you do with the knowledge if I give it to you?"

"I'll marry her."

"Why? Because she's pregnant?" Margo shook her head. "Tara isn't going to marry anybody just to have a father for her child. I would think you'd know that about her by now."

"How can I be expected to know *anything* about her?" he said in sudden exasperation. "During our three weeks together, she never told me one damn thing that I didn't pry out of her first. I didn't even know why she'd dropped out of school until the day before she left Montana."

"And were you any more forthcoming about your life?" Margo asked shrewdly.

"Well, I . . ." He stopped and thought about it for a second. "No, I guess not, but—"

"Did you, even once, ever tell her how much you love her?"

Gage looked, for a moment, as if he'd been pole-axed—*Is it that obvious to everyone?*—and then he smiled ruefully. "I didn't know it myself until she left me," he admitted.

Margo stood eyeing him for a moment more, her brow furrowed with consideration.

"All right," she said, at last. "I'll give you her address." She pulled a piece of paper toward her and wrote it down. Tearing it off the tablet, she folded it in half. "But I'm warning you, Gage Kingston," she said, holding the scrap of paper a moment longer before offering it to him, "if she ends up never speaking to me again, I'm coming after you with an Uzi."

Gage grabbed her upraised hand in one of his, plucking the slip of paper out of her fingers with the other as if he were afraid she'd change her mind and snatch it away again.

"Thank you," he said fervently and, bending his head, he pressed a quick kiss onto the tips of her fingers before he let her go.

12

TARA'S NEW HOUSE was located in a sleepy little community fifty miles outside of the smoggy sprawl of urban Los Angeles. *Fifty miles*, Gage thought, as he pulled to a stop in front of the rambling old house where Tara had holed up. He'd spent six weeks driving himself crazy, wondering where she was and she'd only been fifty lousy miles away!

He sat in the car for a moment after he'd turned the engine off, staring at the charming old Victorian house and wondering why in hell he didn't just get out of the car and go up to the door. He knew she was home. Even from the curb, he could hear the music pouring through the open upstairs windows at the front of the house. There was a brand-new red Saturn sedan sitting on the cracked driveway under the shade of a weathered eucalyptus tree and a lawn sprinkler waving back and forth over a section of the lawn. All he had to do was get out of the car, walk up the meandering stepping-stone path to the porch, knock on the front door and demand that she marry him immediately.

Except . . . what if she said no?

Well, then, he thought, his hands tightening on the steering wheel, he'd remind her of the baby she'd lied to him about. She had to say yes for the sake of the baby.

*"Tara isn't going to marry anybody just to have a fa-
ther for her child."* Margo Melrose's words echoed
through his head as clearly as if she were sitting beside
him in the car.

Gage swore and slammed the heel of his hand against
the wheel, knowing Margo had spoken the truth. If
Tara had completely changed her life in order to avoid
having to tell him about the baby they'd made together, it was a pretty safe bet she wasn't going to marry
him now because of that very same baby.

Would she do it if he admitted that he needed her with
a desperation bordering on madness?

"Hell," he muttered, flinging himself out of the car.
He slammed the door so loud she might have heard it
if it weren't for the raucous country-rock tune filling the
air. He pushed open the white picket gate without
breaking stride, stomped over the stepping-stone path
and up the porch stairs, raised his fist to pound on the
door and . . . couldn't do it.

What if she refused to answer the door? What if she
answered it and then wouldn't let him in? What if— He
felt like a geeky fifteen-year-old math whiz trying to
work up the courage to ask the homecoming queen for
a date.

What if she says no?

Unwilling to be turned down before he even got to the
main question, he dropped his hand to the doorknob
and tested it. It turned under his palm, opening easily,
swinging inward on creaky hinges. *Fate*, he decided,
taking it as a good sign. He stepped inside, closed the
door carefully behind him and followed the golden
voice of Reba McEntire up the stairs and down a nar-

row hall papered in trailing vines and faded blue for-
get-me-nots.

She was standing with her back to the door, wearing
a purple T-shirt and white painter's overalls liberally
sprinkled with varicolored blobs and streaks, smear-
ing yellow paint on the wall of what any fool could see
was destined to become a nursery. Her hair was pulled
up into a high ponytail, the way it had been the first
time he'd kissed her. Her feet were bare and there was
a thick blob of yellow paint dripping down the side of
her right foot. Gage thought she'd never looked more
beautiful. He ached to reach out and touch her, to take
her in his arms and never let her go.

But there were things that had to be said first. Fences
to be mended. Explanations to be made. Apologies to
be offered.

He moved into the room behind her, crossing to
where she had set the tape player on the floor on top of
a canvas drop cloth, and depressed the Power button,
cutting Ms. McEntire off in mid-lament.

Tara swung around with the paint roller in her hand.
Her eyes widened. "Gage."

"You should remember to lock your door, honey.
Anybody could have walked in on you."

"How did you find me?"

"It wasn't easy." He walked over and took the roller
from her upraised hand, stooping to lay it in the roller
pan on the floor. When he straightened he was close
enough to bend his head and kiss her.

She took a step back.

"You shouldn't be working like this in your condition," he said softly, his gaze roving over her face like

a physical touch. "The paint fumes aren't good for you."

"How?" she demanded, ignoring his reference to her condition. Ignoring, too, the almost overpowering urge to throw herself into his arms and beg him to hold her forever.

"Margo told me."

"Margo Melrose? My agent?" Her eyes narrowed suspiciously. "I don't believe you. Margo wouldn't betray me like that."

"It wasn't her fault," Gage said. "I threatened her."

"Margo can't be threatened."

"Actually, I pleaded. She took pity on me."

She turned away from him, crossing her arms over her chest in a self-protective hug, and walked toward the window. "I don't believe that, either."

He watched her standing there in profile to him, looking out over the big tree-shaded front yard. Her face was remote and closed, as if her thoughts were faraway. He ached to touch her, to tell her with his hands and lips how he felt. But she was too distant for that. "I was hoping you'd take pity on me, too," he said softly.

She turned her head to look at him. "I don't know what you mean."

"I mean I want you to marry me."

"No," she said, and turned back toward the window.

"Not even for the baby?"

Especially not for the baby. "You shouldn't believe everything you read in the papers," she said, trying to bluff her way out of it. "There is no baby."

"Then what's all this?"

"It's going to be a guest room when I'm finished painting it."

"With a teddy-bear border?" he asked, nudging the narrow roll of wallpaper on the floor with the toe of his boot.

"There is no baby," she said stubbornly.

"Tara, damn it." He took her by the shoulders, gently but firmly, and turned her to face him. "Don't lie to me. Tell me to get lost or to go to hell or that you hate my guts, but don't lie to me anymore."

She stared up at him silently, afraid to say anything for fear she'd start to cry. She could feel the tears welling up in her eyes, threatening to overflow.

"Is the thought of being pregnant with my baby so terrible?" he asked in an anguished whisper.

"No. No, it's . . ." *It's the most wonderful thing that ever happened to me. And it's breaking my heart.* She a took deep breath and squared her shoulders. "I won't get married just because I'm pregnant, Gage."

"And if I said I love you?"

"Oh, please!" She twisted her shoulders out of his hands and turned away so he wouldn't see her tears fall. "Spare me that, at least."

"I do love you, you know."

"You feel guilty and responsible," she said, shrugging away his hands again as he laid them on her shoulders from behind. "And you're honorable enough not to like feeling that way. But guilt isn't love. And marriage isn't the answer. If we got married you'd just end up hating me for taking your freedom. For taking over your life and changing it into something else."

"Is that the way you feel about me, Tara? Do you hate me for changing your life?"

"No, I don't hate you." She closed her eyes against the tears. "I could never hate you. I lo—" She clamped her lips shut, determined not to say it, but it was too late.

He whirled her around to face him. "Say it, Tara," he demanded, triumphant now. "Damn you, say it."

"I love you. All right?" She all but screamed the words at him. "I love you," she said more quietly. "But I won't marry you just to salve your conscience."

"I didn't ask you to marry me to salve my conscience. I asked you to marry me because I'm in love with you and I'm damn certain I can't live without you."

"Don't," she said, trying to pull away. "Please, don't . . ."

"Marry me, Tara," he urged, pulling her close despite her struggles. He wrapped one arm around her, holding her still, and lifted her chin with his other hand, forcing her to look at him. "Marry me and have my baby," he pleaded. "Have lots of my babies."

"And what about the tabloids?" she whispered, her eyes searching his. "What about all the speculation and gossip about your private life? That isn't going to go away if we get married. What about—"

"To hell with the tabloids," he said savagely. "They don't matter anymore. Not if you love me. Not if you marry me."

"They mattered when you were married to Alyssa."

"You're not Alyssa, damn it! You're nothing like Alyssa," he said, really, truly believing it, deep down inside himself, for the first time. "You're sweet and warm and loving. And if you don't say you'll marry me I'm going to give those scandalmongers the biggest, juiciest scandal of the decade. I'll call a press conference right on your front porch," he threatened. "I'll announce that I'm the father of your 'love child' and that I intend to camp on your doorstep until you make an honest man of me. It'll be the biggest damn media circus you've ever seen."

Tara's eyes went as round as saucers. "You wouldn't."

"I would," he said, and covered her lips with his.

It was a long, wet, eating kiss, a desperate kiss, a kiss of redemption and regret, of apology and adoration, tasting of tears and passions too long denied. Tara surged against him, offering with her lips and her body what she had been afraid to offer with her words. *Take me,* her lips said. *Love me. Never let me go.*

"Never," he said, lifting his mouth from hers to kiss away her tears. "I'll never let you go," he murmured as his lips skimmed her cheeks. "Not for a day. Not for one instant. Never," he vowed, and claimed her mouth again for another long kiss. And when kissing was no longer enough, he lifted her in his arms and carried her out of the nursery and down the hall.

"Here," she said, indicating the door to her bedroom.

He carried her over the threshold like a bride and set her on her feet on the floor by the old-fashioned tester bed. He undressed her slowly, with the same care and reverence he would have shown if she had been wearing fragile white lace instead of painter's overalls.

"They're fuller already," he said, gently touching the lush curve of her breast as they lay naked together on top of the flower-strewn quilt. "Is it all right?"

She covered his hand with hers, pressing it against her in answer. "It's better than all right."

"And this?" he asked, brushing his thumb over her distended nipple.

She arched into his touch.

"And this?" he asked, bending his head to suckle her breast.

She moaned softly and clenched her hands in his hair to hold him closer.

"Your breasts are so much more sensitive now," he murmured, fascinated by the changes in her body.

"Everything's more sensitive now."

"Here?"

"Yes."

"And here?"

"Oh, yes."

"And here?"

"Oh . . . oh my, yes," she moaned as his fingers slid into the wet, hot center of her. "Oh, yes, Gage. *Please.*"

She became a bit frantic then, impatient with his tender teasing and soft touches. She rolled toward him, aching to be filled, aching to have *him* fill her, and threw a slender thigh over his hip. Tilting her pelvis, she rubbed against him in unmistakable invitation. He entered her eagerly, as anxious for total communion as she was, and they made love lying face-to-face, with soft sighs and lingering caresses and deep, moist kisses that went on forever. He rolled her onto her back at the last, rising above her to balance himself on his hands, thrusting slow and deep until she came apart beneath him. And then he lowered himself and slipped his arms under her, holding on tight while his own climax thundered through him.

"My love." He sighed into her hair a moment later. "My love. I'll never let you go again."

THE TABLOIDS HAD A field day with the wedding. It was held on Pierce's lavish Beverly Hills estate with a select guest list sworn to secrecy. Claire and Margo attended the bride, attired in ice blue and lavender sheaths, respectively. Pierce and Hans Ostfield stood up for Gage. The ceremony itself was held under a huge white silk canopy to prevent the circling helicopters from taking pictures. Extra security patrolled the grounds to keep out crashers, although no one could stop the paparazzi from snapping pictures of the guests as they drove up to the gates.

The next morning's tabloids had pictures of Bruce Willis and Demi Moore, Tom Cruise and Nicole Kidman, Goldie Hawn and Kurt Russell, Kevin Costner and his wife Cindy, the Spielbergs, the Gregory Pecks, the Douglases and the Bridges, as well as the less recognizable faces of agents, directors and movie technicians of all kinds. It was later discovered that the fuzzy, out-of-focus pictures of the bride and groom had been taken by one of the caterer's assistants with a hidden camera.

Tara Channing Weds Father Of Her Love Child, the headlines read. One paper mocked the fact that Tara— the most notorious "other woman" since Jean Harlow—had worn white satin and Elise Gage's antique lace veil. Another suggested that Gage had been blackmailed into marrying her, citing the usual "reliable sources" to back up the ridiculous allegation. A third swore that her bulging stomach—though still practically nonexistent four months into her pregnancy—had ruined the line of her wedding gown.

Gage and Tara used every single one of the scandal sheets to start a roaring blaze in the fireplace. Then they toasted each other with vintage champagne and made love until there was nothing left of the fire but a few glowing embers.

TARA FEARS LOSING Gorgeous Gage To Hawaiian Honey, the headlines screamed two months later when it was revealed that, despite her advanced pregnancy, Tara would be accompanying Gage on location to Hawaii to film a Hallmark Hall of Fame movie. According to the tabloids, Tara was so unsure of Gage's fidelity that she'd set aside her own career to follow her husband everywhere in order to keep an eye on him.

"You could go back to work after the baby's born, you know," Gage said as he rubbed coconut-scented sunscreen on the swollen mound of his wife's belly. They were getting some sun on their own private Hawaiian lanai during a break in the shooting. "The studio would be thrilled to get Jessica back. And I know Claire has a couple of scripts she'd like you to consider. She says you're going to be very much in demand when *The Promise* comes out next Christmas."

"Nope," Tara said lazily, her eyes closed as she savored her husband's loving attentions. "I have no intention of ever getting in front of a camera again."

"Not even for me?"

"Well—" she opened her eyes and gave him her slanted, sideways look "—maybe for you. Privately. *After* the baby's born."

TARA ATTENDS PREMIERE OF *The Promise* Pregnant With Triplets, the tabloids said the following December, offering two pages of full-color pictures of her with her enlarged belly as proof positive. She was nine months and two weeks into her pregnancy—a fact that even her custom-designed Valentino gown couldn't hide as she traversed the red carpet between the stretch limo and the door of the theater on the arm of her solicitous husband.

People did an article on the premiere the following week, slanting it more toward the astounding box-office receipts of *The Promise* rather than the fact that Tara Channing and Gage Kingston had been forced to leave in the middle of the movie to go to the hospital.

THIRTY-SIX HOURS OF EXCRUCIATING LABOR, the tabloids announced as Tara lay in utter contentment nursing her day-old baby boy with her husband in adoring attendance.

Tara sighed and smiled, lifting her lashes to look at Gage. "So," she murmured, "how do you feel about being the man in the 'other woman's' life so far?"

He reached out and brushed her hair back, then trailed his fingers down the creamy slope of her breast to caress his tiny son's rosy cheek. "You're not the 'other woman,'" he said, smiling at her with his heart in his eyes. "You're the only woman."

Coming Attractions

DON'T MISS THE next two books in the blockbuster Hollywood Dynasty miniseries! Find out how the Kingston family continues to thrive amid the troubles and triumphs of being silver-screen legends.

In *Just Another Pretty Face* (#459), action-film star and sex symbol Pierce Kingston vetoes his overprotective sister's idea that he needs a bodyguard, despite the threatening letters he's been receiving. But he does an about-face when he meets his new "shadow"—a tall, gorgeous brunette. Nikki Martinelli doesn't trust good-looking men. But Pierce is determined to get past her defenses—even if she *is* a martial arts expert! Coming in September 1993.

A hot director melts cool Claire Kingston's icy heart in *The Right Direction* (#467). Watch for it in November.

Take 4 bestselling love stories FREE

Plus get a FREE surprise gift!

Special Limited-time Offer

Mail to Harlequin Reader Service®

3010 Walden Avenue
P.O. Box 1867
Buffalo, N.Y. 14269-1867

YES! Please send me 4 free Harlequin Temptation® novels and my free surprise gift. Then send me 4 brand-new novels every month, which I will receive before they appear in bookstores. Bill me at the low price of $2.44 each plus 25¢ delivery and applicable sales tax, if any.* That's the complete price and—compared to the cover prices of $2.99 each—quite a bargain! I understand that accepting the books and gift places me under no obligation ever to buy any books. I can always return a shipment and cancel at any time. Even if I never buy another book from Harlequin, the 4 free books and the surprise gift are mine to keep forever.

142 BPA AJHR

Name	(PLEASE PRINT)
Address	Apt. No.
City	State	Zip

This offer is limited to one order per household and not valid to present Harlequin Temptation® subscribers.
*Terms and prices are subject to change without notice. Sales tax applicable in N.Y.

HARLEQUIN®

Temptation®

NEW AUTHOR

THE VOICES OF TOMORROW TODAY

Sensuous, bold, sometimes controversial, Harlequin Temptation novels are stories of women today—the attitudes, desires, lives and language of the nineties.

The distinctive voices of our authors is the hallmark of Temptation. We are proud to announce two new voices are joining the spectacular Temptation lineup.

Kate Hoffman, *INDECENT EXPOSURE*, #456, August 1993

Jennifer Crusie, *MANHUNTING*, #463, October 1993

Tune in to the hottest station on the romance dial—Temptation!

Dear Reader,

We hope you enjoyed Gage and Tara's story and are looking forward to the upcoming books about Pierce and Claire. We value your opinions and invite you to write to us telling us what you like about Hollywood Dynasty. Do you find the sex, sins and behind-the-scenes glimpses of the film industry interesting? Why or why not? What made you pick up this book? What elements did you find most appealing in the story and why? Along with your letter, please answer the following questionnaire and mail both today to:

Customer Opinion Center
P.O. Box 1387
Buffalo, NY 14240-9990

Thanks for sharing your opinions with us.

Birgit Davis-Todd
Harlequin Temptation

1. How likely are you to purchase another Temptation novel next month?
   ☐ Definitely will purchase   ☐ Probably will not purchase
   ☐ Probably will purchase   ☐ Definitely will not purchase

2. Which Harlequin series is your favorite? _____

3. What are your three favorite television programs? _____
_____

4. Where do you usually buy romance paperbacks?
   ☐ Supermarket   ☐ Discount Store   ☐ Mail Subscription
   ☐ Drugstore   ☐ Used Bookstore   ☐ Bookstore

5. Please indicate your age range:
   ☐ under 18   ☐ 25 to 34   ☐ 50 to 64
   ☐ 18 to 24   ☐ 35 to 49   ☐ 65 or older